Suddenly, D.J. stopped dead still. "Listen!"

Alfred cocked his head. "Sounds like somebody crying!"

"Couldn't be Mr. Zeering," D.J. said softly. "What would he have to cry about?"

The boys traced the sound around the corner of the rough-hewn lumber that made up the little home. The hermit's back was to the boys. Zeke Zeering was crouched under a small young cedar with wide-spreading branches.

"Mr. Zeering?" D.J. called softly, hearing the sobbing sounds.

Slowly, the old hermit turned around, holding a short-handled shovel. There were tearstains down his cheeks. He spoke with a broken voice. "They done killed my dog!"

LEE RODDY is a best-selling author of more than 50 books. He lives in the Sierra Nevada Mountains of California and devotes his time to writing books and public speaking. He is a co-writer of the book which became the TV series, "The Life and Times of Grizzly Adams."

Born on an Illinois farm and reared on a California ranch, Lee Roddy grew up around hunters and trail hounds. As a boy, he began writing animal stories. He spent lots of time reading about dogs, horses, and other animals. These stories shaped his thinking and values before he went to Hollywood to write professionally. His Christian commitment later turned his writing talents to books like this one.

This is the ninth book in the D.J. Dillon Adventure Series.

The Secret of Mad River

LEE RODDY

VICTOR BOOKS
A DIVISION OF SCRIPTURE PRESS PUBLICATIONS INC.
USA CANADA ENGLAND

THE D.J. DILLON ADVENTURE SERIES

THE HAIR-PULLING BEAR DOG
THE BEAR CUB DISASTER
DOOGER, THE GRASSHOPPER HOUND
THE GHOST DOG OF STONEY RIDGE
MAD DOG OF LOBO MOUNTAIN
THE LEGEND OF THE WHITE RACCOON
THE MYSTERY OF THE BLACK HOLE MINE
GHOST OF THE MOANING MANSION
THE SECRET OF MAD RIVER
ESCAPE DOWN THE RAGING RAPIDS

4 5 6 7 8 9 10 11 12 13 Printing/Year 00 99 98 97 96

All Scripture quotations are from the *King James Version*.

Library of Congress Catalog Card Number: 88-60212
ISBN: 1-56476-510-5

CONTENTS

1. Coming of the Stray Dog Pack   7
2. When Troubles Multiply   8
3. Tragedy for an Old Powder Monkey   27
4. A Mean Dog Named Boog   38
5. The Newspaper Editor's Surprise   44
6. A New Danger   52
7. Kathy Meets the Brindle   63
8. Clue in a Town about to Drown   70
9. Hero Worsens   79
10. A Terrible Sight in the Meadow   86
11. Buried Alive!   96
12. The Other Side of Nothing   107
13. Easter Sunday   116
    Life in Stoney Ridge   121

To Brian Russell,
with deep gratitude
for being my
writing mentor and friend

Chapter One

COMING OF THE STRAY DOG PACK

D.J. Dillon's blond head snapped up sharply when he heard the distant yelp of pain. His tall, slender body stiffened as he cocked his head to listen. He spun away from his best friend, Alfred Milford, and the dime store clerk. She was stapling a receipt onto the paper sack containing two Easter cards D.J. had bought.

The second cry of pain jerked the boy into action. He ran toward the store's glass front door, not hearing the clerk call that he'd forgotten his package.

Alfred, running behind D.J., exclaimed, "That sounds like your dog!"

"It is!" D.J. sprinted through the small store, his heavy shoes clumping loudly on the old wooden floor.

As D.J. shoved the door open, he heard vicious snarling down the street and around the corner. D.J. broke into a wild run.

"Dogfight!" Alfred cried. "Some dogs must have jumped Hero!"

"And he's tied up!" D.J. puffed. He sprinted down the sidewalk of Indian Springs' steep main street. He was so intent on reaching the corner that he didn't notice the beautiful April morning in the Mother Lode* foothills. D.J. dodged a few early Saturday morning shoppers just as he reached the corner of Main Street and Forty-Niner Avenue.

"Look out!" Alfred called.

Three dogs dashed around the corner from Forty-Niner Avenue, almost knocking D.J. down. He leaped toward the red adobe* brick building to let the dogs pass. D.J. was only subconsciously aware that two were large animals. The third was a smaller brindled* pit bull terrier with blood on its muzzle.

As the dogs ran on, D.J. shoved himself away from the wall and right into two people racing around the corner. As they collided, D.J. caught a glimpse of a stocky man with long, shaggy hair and an untidy, full beard. Beside the man was a long-haired boy about D.J.'s age.

"Whoops! Sorry!" D.J. exclaimed, fighting to keep his balance so he wouldn't fall off the high concrete sidewalk into the street.

"Why don't you watch where you're going?" the man demanded angrily without stopping.

"Yeah!" the long-haired boy added, shoving D.J. back against the adobe brick wall.

D.J. flailed his arms to keep from losing his

*You can find an explanation of the starred words under "Life in Stoney Ridge" on pages 121–126.

balance. When he regained it, he saw the man and
the boy disappearing down the street after the dogs.

Alfred touched his friend's jacket sleeve. "You
OK, D.J.?"

"Yes! Come on! Let's see what's happened to
Hero!"

D.J. swung wide around the corner and glanced
ahead to where he'd left his mixed breed dog tied
to a bicycle rack. Halfway down the block, the boy
saw a terrible sight.

His little shaggy-haired, reddish-brown dog was
stretched out on the sidewalk in a widening puddle
of blood. A girl with reddish hair was kneeling beside
him and sobbing. Kathy Stagg, D.J., and Alfred all at-
tended the same school in nearby Stoney Ridge.

In a moment, D.J. knelt beside his dog. Hero
whined in recognition and tried to raise his head,
but he couldn't.

"What happened, Kathy?" D.J. demanded, his
blue eyes quickly checking the dog's torn ears,
muzzle, shoulders, ribs, and flanks.

The boy had seen Hero hurt before, especially
from tackling a wild bear. But D.J. had never seen
such terrible wounds as Hero had just suffered.

"I—I—" Kathy tried to answer, but her voice
broke. With an effort, she gained control. Words
poured out of her in an anguished stream.

"I was way down the block when I saw three
dogs jump Hero. I yelled at them, but they didn't
pay any attention. Hero's leash was so short he
couldn't get away or defend himself much!

"Then a man and a kid ran up and started kicking. At first, I thought they were trying to boot the

other dogs away from Hero! Then I realized they were kicking *him* as if it were his fault!"

D.J. glanced up at Kathy, his blue eyes blazing. "They *what?*"

Kathy nodded vigorously, her reddish hair cascading down both sides of her head. "I ran toward them and yelled for them to stop! The dogs took off toward the corner—the way you and Alfred came! Then the man and boy ran off the same way. You must have seen them!"

The boy leaped to his feet, sudden anger burning through his body. He glanced at Alfred, who nodded. Now D.J. understood why the brindled pit bull terrier's muzzle had been bloody. D.J. wanted to run after the man, boy, and three dogs, but that would have to wait. D.J. felt hot tears forming in his eyes.

Alfred spoke softly. "Three dogs to one! Plus the man and the kid! And Hero tied with that short leash chain!"

D.J. didn't seem to hear. "I've got to get Hero to a vet, fast!" He glanced wildly around, vaguely aware that a small crowd had silently gathered to stare down at the hurt animal. "Where's your father, Kathy?"

D.J., Alfred, and Hero had ridden down from Stoney Ridge to the county seat at Indian Springs with Kathy and her father. They had split up to shop, agreeing to meet back at the car in an hour.

"He went to the hardware store while I was looking at an Easter outfit in the window next door. Oh, here he comes!"

Through eyes misting with unwanted tears, D.J. glimpsed a giant of a man pushing gently but firmly through the spectators. In his cowboy hat and boots, Paul Stagg seemed nearly seven feet tall.

Brother Paul Stagg was the lay preacher of the only church in the small lumbering town where D.J., Alfred, and the Staggs lived.

Brother Paul's voice rumbled up from his massive chest like distant thunder as he bent over the boy and dog. "Let me see, please!"

D.J. stepped aside. Kathy's father knelt in faded blue jeans. He ran experienced eyes over Hero's body. Brother Paul looked up at D.J. "He's hurt bad, looks like. I'll get the car and we'll run him over to the vet's."

D.J. nodded, unable to speak. As Brother Paul jogged away, D.J. knelt and began speaking softly to Hero.

"It'll be OK, Boy! We'll get you patched up! You'll be out chasing bears again in no time! You'll see!"

But D.J. didn't really believe that. From a lifetime of living in California's Sierra Nevada Mountains, the boy knew that Hero might never again run a trail. He might not even live. . . .

D.J. shook his head to stop the terrible thought. He glanced up at Alfred, seeing him through the thickening mist of scalding tears.

"I shouldn't have left him alone!"

Alfred pushed his thick glasses up with a characteristic motion of his right thumb. "You had no choice, D.J. The law doesn't allow dogs in stores. He had to be tied here."

Kathy sniffed loudly. "Is—is Hero going to die?"

D.J. looked at her for a long moment, unable to trust his voice. He was afraid it would crack, and he'd lose control of his tears too.

Alfred answered for him. "Hero's tough, Kathy! He'll make it! Remember when that outlaw bear* almost got D.J. and you, and Hero saved you both? And the hermit of Mad River nursed him back to health?"

D.J.'s eyes were so filled with hot mists that he couldn't see Kathy clearly, but he thought she nodded. The boy glanced down helplessly at his pet, frustrated because he couldn't do anything to ease the little dog's pain or stop the flow of blood from his many wounds.

D.J. felt Alfred lightly touch him on the shoulder. "It'll be OK," his friend said softly. "Brother Paul's car is coming down the street."

D.J. could no longer hold back the scalding tears that seeped from the corners of his eyes. He bent far over his pet until his forehead almost touched the dog's ribs. D.J. let the tears mingle with the bright-red blood on the dog's body.

"Don't die, Hero! Please don't die!"

At the small animal hospital, D.J. suffered mentally over the next couple of hours. He paced the narrow waiting room in front of the counter. Time and time again he glanced down the hallway where a man in a white smock had taken Hero.

D.J. was vaguely aware of a medicine smell, and of dogs barking somewhere deep in the building. The boy didn't really notice the young woman receptionist behind the counter, or Brother Paul, Alfred, and Kathy sitting nearby, trying to read old magazines.

"Please, Lord!" D.J. barely whispered the words as he stood in front of a color poster showing many breeds of dogs. "Don't let him die!"

The boy's anguished prayer was snapped off when a nice-looking man and a well-dressed teenage boy entered the waiting room. *Father and son,* D.J. thought. The boy carried a calico cat* to the counter.

"We found this cat beside the highway. We think a car must have hit it," the man explained to the receptionist. "It doesn't seem to be hurt too much, but we brought it in to have it checked over."

Kathy stood and whispered to D.J., "Now there are some nice people!"

D.J. was too anxious about Hero to reply, but without knowing why, D.J. instantly disliked the man and boy. That was unusual for D.J., so he studied the people at the counter.

The kid was about the same age and height as D.J., but had dark, wavy hair instead of pale, straight blond hair like D.J. had. The kid's dark eyes turned from the cat to rest on Kathy. The boy smiled at her, and she smiled back. D.J. felt an even keener sense of dislike for the boy.

The receptionist struck a small bell on the counter, and the same white-jacketed man who'd taken Hero away came out of a side room. He gently carried the cat into the room and closed the door.

D.J. heard the man who had come in with the cat give the receptionist information for a form she was filling out.

"Norvell Thorkell. San Francisco. This is my son, Thad."

Thad turned from smiling at Kathy to acknowledge the introduction to the receptionist. She nodded and asked more questions.

D.J. noticed that Thad was nicely dressed in tan

slacks and matching loafers, pale checked sport shirt, and a brown suede jacket. It was missing the middle button of the three on the right sleeve.

Norvell Thorkell was about six feet tall, clean-shaven and well-dressed in a dark-gray suit with just a hint of a pattern.

The son excused himself and walked over to Kathy. "Hi," he said, smiling. "I'm Thad Thorkell."

D.J. turned away as Kathy introduced herself, her father, and Alfred. D.J. stared down the hallway where Hero had been carried. He heard Kathy explaining about his dog being attacked by a pack of dogs.

D.J. didn't hear any more. An attractive woman in a short white jacket walked briskly down the hallway to face D.J.

"You must be the owner of the little shaggy-haired dog. I'm Dr. Barner. I've just finished examining your dog."

D.J. was aware that Brother Paul, Alfred, and Kathy had moved in beside him. The new kid rejoined his father at the counter.

"How is he?" D.J. asked anxiously.

Dr. Barner shook her short, dark hair. "There are so many wounds, he's in shock from tissue trauma.* He also has hypovalemia shock—that's a drop in blood pressure—because of tissue and blood loss."

She paused, then added, "He must have been involved with a pit bull."

When D.J. nodded, the vet continued, "It's characteristic for them to try breaking the two bones in the front leg. The pit bull tries to cripple his opponent that way. But don't blame the breed—it's the owner's responsibility to train the dog properly. Pit bulls have had such bad publicity!"

D.J. interrupted. "How—how bad is Hero hurt?"

"Both of your dog's front legs are broken. But cracked bones heal well, and he'll be able to run a trail again—if he survives his other wounds."

D.J. swallowed hard, unable to ask what that meant. But Brother Paul asked it for him. The lay pastor's deep bass voice echoed softly through the room.

"How serious are those?"

"The attackers didn't miss much except the jugular vein. Hero has a chest puncture and tears and lacerations everywhere. Several severe wounds show that while one dog worked on the front quarters, others attacked sides and rear.

"I've aspirated* the chest puncture so he can breathe and ordered a chest X ray. We've stopped the obvious bleeding and started antibiotics.*"

D.J. didn't really understand the meaning of all the vet's words, but the boy had a terrible sense of his little dog being in great danger. D.J. wanted to speak, but couldn't. He felt Brother Paul's big hand on his elbow.

The lay pastor rumbled, "I used to be a bear hunter, so I've seen dogs hurt bad. Are you saying that Hero's going to be all right?"

Dr. Barner replied cautiously. "He'll be in shock for four or five hours. Then we'll do whatever else we can. But he won't be out of danger for about seventy-two hours."

"Three days!" Alfred said softly.

"If . . . " D.J. found his voice. "I mean,
when . . . he makes it that long, then what?"

"He'll be through the danger unless serious infection sets in. But let's hope that won't happen."

"Can—can I see him?"

"Not right now. After such a trauma, dogs usually
don't know much of what's going on for twelve to
eighteen hours. But he's a tough little fighter—I can
tell that because his body is covered with old scars."

Alfred explained proudly, "He's a hair-pulling
bear dog!* He got those wounds from fighting Ol'
Satchelfoot* the outlaw bear!"

"Oh?" The vet nodded. "I remember that story! It
was in the local newspaper."

D.J.'s mind leaped back to when Hero had saved
his life and Kathy's life from the renegade bear. At
first, the boy thought Ol' Satchelfoot had killed the
dog and carried off his body. Only later did D.J.
learn that a hermit had found the dog, more dead
than alive, and nursed him back to health. Surely
Hero had a better chance now because a vet was
caring for him.

The vet concluded. "We'll take good care of him.
You get some rest and check with me tomorrow.
OK?"

D.J. nodded but couldn't speak.

Brother Paul said, "We're obliged to you,
Doctor."

D.J. wasn't thinking about anything except his little dog getting well. The boy started out the front
door, but stopped and went back when he realized
Brother Paul had paused at the receptionist's
counter. The preacher pulled out his wallet.

The boy suddenly realized he hadn't even thought about the need for money to care for his dog.

D.J. whispered, "I'll pay you back as soon as I can."

"Forget it," the lay preacher rumbled.

As they walked out, D.J. saw the nice-looking Thorkells were just getting into their car. Thad waved at Kathy, and she waved back.

Thad called through the open front passenger side window, "Sure hope the dog gets well fast."

"Thanks," Kathy said. "I hope the same for the cat."

D.J. turned away quickly. His blue eyes traveled on toward the far end of the small animal emergency hospital. Inside that long, low building, the best dog in the world was suffering—maybe dying! Hero had never hurt anybody in his whole life, and he didn't deserve to be hurt!

Blood scalded through D.J.'s body with an anger he'd never known. He hadn't ever wanted revenge for anything, but a surge of blazing fury made the boy whisper fiercely aloud, "Hang on, Hero! Hang on! I'll find the ones who hurt you! Then I'll make them pay!"

Chapter Two

WHEN TROUBLES MULTIPLY

After reporting the incident to the sheriff's office, D.J. was driven home by the lay preacher. D.J.'s father and grandfather were sitting on the top step of the Dillon's front porch when Brother Paul dropped off the boy.

Dad Dillon glanced up from fitting a new handle onto a double-bitted ax head.* D.J.'s father waved a powerful, work-hardened hand at the lay pastor who waved back and drove off.

Grandpa Dillon shifted what he called his Irish shillelagh* to ease his arthritic hip. D.J. sensed the older man was probing the boy's face with sharp, discerning eyes.

"Howdy, D.J.," Grandpa said. He peered over the top of his wire-rimmed bifocals. "Where's your dog?"

D.J. saw his father stop his work, suddenly aware that something unusual must have happened.

D.J. took a deep breath before he spoke. "Hero

got hurt," he replied. He had determined not to lose control of his emotions. He walked to the garden hose, turned it on, and carried the end over to the high curb. He washed his hands vigorously. He heard his father and grandfather leave the porch steps and quickly walk up beside him.

"What happened?" Dad demanded.

"And *how?*" Grandpa asked. His voice was gentle as D.J.'s mother's voice had been. A long time ago the boy's mother had been killed in an auto accident.

The front screen door squeaked open and D.J.'s stepmother and stepsister came onto the porch. The boy saw Pris, the nine-year-old girl, start to speak. Two Mom, as D.J. called his father's new wife, held up a hand for silence. Mother and daughter stood silently listening.

D.J. stared at the lawn. In a soft voice he explained what had happened in Indian Springs. He dropped the hose on the new spring lawn and dried his hands on his pants legs, aware that his eyes were misting up again.

Priscilla cried, "Oh, D.J.! That's *awful!* Is Hero going to *die?*"

The boy turned away. The swollen knot in his throat kept him silent. He stared unseeingly across the little lumbering town of Stoney Ridge. The high Sierra Nevada Mountains, heavy with snow, soared sharply upward to the east.

Dad Dillon asked, "You don't know the people who owned the dogs?"

"Never saw any of them before." He turned back to face his family. "The man was about your age, Dad. Or Brother Paul's. Only bearded and long-haired. The kid was close to my age. Probably father and son."

"The dogs?" Grandpa prompted.

"Two were big. One was a police dog mix; mostly black. The other was maybe a mastiff cross.* The smaller was a brindle-colored pit bull. Had a white blaze on his head and a white spot on his chest."

Two Mom's hands fluttered about as they always did when she was excited or nervous. "We'd better call the sheriff's office right away! Those dogs are dangerous! That could have been a child they attacked! And people who'd kick a poor defenseless dog when he was tied—well!"

D.J. replied dully, "Brother Paul stopped by the sheriff's office, and I told them."

Grandpa put a thin arm around D.J.'s shoulders. "D.J., I recken you can rest easy, seeing as how the deputies will take care of things now."

The boy shook his head. "It's not that easy, Grandpa. They're all busy with some kind of bomb threat investigation."

"Bomb threat?" Two Mom exclaimed. "Mercy! What would anyone bomb around here?"

D.J. shrugged. "Something about the new dam being built on Mad River."

Dad drove his right fist into the calloused left palm with a loud smack. "I knew that dam would cause trouble! All them environmental-type people coming up here to protest with their signs and things!"

D.J. said, "I don't like to see the river dammed up either, but the dam's being built, and nobody's going to stop it."

"Unless," Grandpa said quietly, his false teeth

clicking, "there's somebody out in these mountains who's mad enough to really blow it up."

"Anyway," D.J. said, dismissing the subject, "all the deputies are tied up on that. But they will send the animal control officer out to see me when he has time."

"Good!" Two Mom exclaimed. "Then you can rest easy! Just wait for your dog to get well."

D.J. shook his head firmly. "No, they hurt my dog *real* bad. I can't wait for the animal control officer to come out here. I want to find them myself."

Dad exclaimed, "Now see here, young man! If those people and their dogs hurt Hero like you say they did, what makes you think they won't do the same to you? Stay out of this! Let the law handle it!"

Two Mom came down from the porch to stand by the boy. "Besides, we must remember what God's Word says: ' "Vengeance is Mine; I will re-pay," saith the Lord' " (Romans 12:19).

D.J. was usually a very mild-mannered boy, but he was so upset his voice was sharp. "God also says He demands justice!"

Two Mom said quietly, "I don't remember that verse, but if it is in the Bible, I'd think that means justice for people, D.J."

"Well, I want it for my dog too! And I'm going to see that it happens!" He ran into the house and to his room so nobody could see his tears.

* * * * *

D.J. awoke the next morning with a dull ache inside. It was barely daylight when he pulled on his robe and slippers. He padded quietly down the silent hallway to the kitchen.

He closed the door and looked up the veterinarian hospital's number. He dialed and impatiently waited while the phone rang a dozen times. Finally, a male voice, probably a teenager, answered.

"Hello? I'm D.J. Dillon and I brought my little dog in yesterday morning. His name's Hero. He'd been kicked by some people and bitten by some dogs. How's he doing?"

D.J. heard a yawn on the other end of the line. "I'm just the night kid, but I know which dog you mean."

"How is he?" D.J. repeated anxiously.

"You'd have to ask Dr. Barner."

"Is she there?"

"No."

"Can't you give me any idea of how he looks?"

There was a hesitation. "Well, he's not doing too hot."

The boy's heart plunged like a chunk of lead in his chest. "You mean—he's—dying?"

"You'll have to ask the doc, and she won't be in for a few hours."

D.J. was so sick at heart he didn't even hang up the phone. He was vaguely aware of Two Mom reaching over him and replacing the telephone receiver. D.J. hadn't heard her come into the room.

"Bad news, D.J.?" she asked, tightening the belt on her gray robe.

Wordlessly, he nodded, feeling frustration and anger rise inside him. Didn't anybody really care about Hero? The kid on the phone had yawned; the dog wasn't that important to him. Where was the vet? She should be in the office looking after Hero!

Maybe he was dying!

His stepmother said gently, "There's nothing you can do. Why don't you go back to bed for a while? I'll wake you in time for Sunday School and church."

D.J. shook his head. "I don't feel like going to church today."

"You'll feel better after we get there."

"No, I won't! I won't *ever* feel better until I find those people and their dogs! Especially the brindle!"

"Now, D.J., that's not like you!"

The boy didn't want to talk about it. He changed the subject. "Is it OK if I walk over to Alfred's house?"

"He is probably still asleep."

"I'll wake him up! Anyway, I can't sit around here or in church! Not today!"

"D.J., I don't want you trying to find those people or their dogs! Let the law handle that!"

D.J. interrupted. "I'll be careful! Honest! I'll just try to find out who they are or where they live — that's all!"

Two Mom seemed doubtful. "You'll call the sheriff's office and let them handle it?"

The boy hesitated, then reluctantly nodded.

"Well, we'd better talk to your father about this. Besides, you couldn't do anything now. This is the Lord's Day. You'll have to wait until tomorrow — if your father will let you."

D.J.'s frustration boiled up instantly. "Aw, Two Mom! Tomorrow's a school day! I can't go looking then!"

"No, there's no school next week; it's Easter

vacation. Remember?"

"I forgot." D.J. suddenly remembered the cards he'd left at the dime store in Indian Springs. He'd have to get a ride down to the county seat to get them.

Two Mom patted his arm. "You've got time. Well, I'm going back to bed for a while. I suggest you do the same."

"I can't sleep," he protested. "Been awake most of the night."

"Then study your Sunday School lesson quietly until the rest of the family wakes up. Then we'll all go to church together."

Nearly an hour later, D.J. was trying to study in his room when he heard the phone ring. He threw on his robe and ran barefoot down the hall to the kitchen.

Probably the vet! he told himself. *With good news, I hope!*

He snatched the receiver off the hook and said "hello." A man's voice came over the line.

"D.J.? This is Mr. Kersten. I'm glad I caught you before your family left for church."

Mr. Kersten was editor of *The Timbergold Gazette* in Indian Springs where D.J. was a stringer.* D.J. thought maybe Mr. Kersten had heard about his dog and was calling to say how sorry he was. Instead, the editor went straight to business.

"You remember that old hermit who lives on Mad River?"

"Mr. Zeering? Sure! He once saved my dog's—"

"I remember!" the editor interrupted. "I know he's an ornery old cuss who'd just as soon run people off his land as look at them. But he likes you.

That's why I thought of asking you to interview him instead of sending one of my staff reporters."

D.J. was puzzled. "Interview him? What for?"

"Well, you know that when the new dam is built, the water that's impounded* will back up and bury his old shack along with that town of Yellow Dog."

"I knew about the town, but not about Mr. Zeering's place. I thought he was too high up the canyon."

"His will be the last dwelling drowned."

D.J. didn't feel like writing about anything. As an independent contractor, D.J. knew Mr. Kersten couldn't order him to do the story the way an editor could a staff reporter. The boy started to explain, but the editor broke in.

"I need that story by five o'clock Tuesday afternoon. That's why I called this morning when I got the idea of sending you. You've got a tape recorder, haven't you?

"Yes. Dad bought one at a garage sale. Battery operated."

"Good! Tape your conversation with the old man. Then write the story and get it in to me by Tuesday."

An idea hit D.J. Going to see the hermit would give the boy an opportunity to ask questions of people he met. He didn't know of any pit bulls in these mountains, especially a brindle. Maybe D.J. could get a lead that would help him find the long-haired people and the three dogs.

D.J. said, "What do you want me to ask Mr. Zeering?"

"Make it a feature story, not just hard facts. Try to get the man's feelings. Ask what he thinks about losing the home where he's lived all these years. How he feels about the dam going in, and the town of Yellow Dog being sixty feet under water. OK?"

The boy hesitated, wondering if his father would let him go for fear D.J. might search for the brindle.

The editor misunderstood the boy's hesitation. "Tell you what, D.J.—if you make the deadline, I'll not only pay your stringer's rate, but I'll throw in a nice cash bonus too! What d'ya say?"

Suddenly, D.J. saw a way to earn some of the money needed to pay for Hero's treatment.

"I'll ask my Dad, Mr. Kersten."

"Great! Call me back. I'm at home."

D.J. met his father coming out of the bathroom. The boy quickly explained about the editor's request and the offer of a bonus.

Dad frowned. "You won't go running off somewhere else, looking for those dogs?"

"I won't go out of my way."

"Well, you still owe Brother Paul, and you'll need money for the rest of the vet bill. I guess it's OK."

D.J. hurried to the telephone and relayed his father's message to the editor. Then D.J. thought of something else.

"Mr. Kersten, I was at the sheriff's office yesterday and heard something about a bomb threat to the dam. What's that all about?"

"I'll fill you in when you bring me that feature on the hermit. Don't let me down, you hear?"

"I won't," D.J. promised, and hung up the phone.

At once, a funny feeling seeped over the boy. He shivered. He didn't know why, but somehow he sensed that he was about to run into awful danger.

TRAGEDY FOR AN OLD POWDER MONKEY

The scary feeling of danger stayed with D.J. as the family drove to the little community church. When the sedan eased into the parking lot, D.J. saw the familiar small frame building with its short steeple. The steeple was filled with thousands of woodpecker holes. The steep corrugated* metal roof helped resist fires and made winter snows slide off.

Priscilla asked, "Who's that with Kathy?"

D.J. recognized Thad Thorkell, the boy who had carried the calico cat into the animal hospital. He was smiling at Kathy, and she was smiling back.

"I think his name's Thorkell," D.J. replied, glowering at the stranger. "From San Francisco."

"In that case," Two Mom said, getting out of the car, "we'd better all go over and make him welcome to Stoney Ridge."

"Aw, Two Mom!" D.J. protested.

Two Mom insisted and Dad backed her up. The

Dillon family walked up to Kathy and the new boy for introductions. Thad wore an expensive, hand-tailored dark suit, white shirt, and subdued blue tie.

Kathy pointed to each in turn. "This is Mr. and Mrs. Dillon, Grandpa Dillon, and Priscilla and D.J."

Dad shook hands with the new boy. "Your family with you, Thad?"

"That's my father, Norvell, over there talking with the preacher."

Kathy beamed. "Guess what? Thad and his father are environmentalists, just like me! Thad's even been a protester with signs and everything."

D.J. didn't much like the new kid though it was hard to say why. "What'd you protest?"

"Oh, lots of things. Mostly against damming the white river rapids. It's destroying the natural environment and impacting the whole area. Like Mad River. That's why we're here."

D.J. thought the kid sounded as if he'd read a lot about the subject. Another thought hit D.J. He wondered if the Thorkells hated the dam enough to threaten blowing it up. But D.J. also caught a hopeful sign in the new kid's words.

"Then you're not going to live here?" D.J. asked.

"Oh, no! We're just here for a demonstration. But since this is Palm Sunday, we wanted to go to church. We always do that wherever we go."

D.J. had mixed feelings. It was good Thad and his father were only visitors, but it wasn't likely that anyone who went to church would threaten to blow up a dam. Still, D.J. didn't much like the new kid.

"Well," Dad Dillon said, "there's the bell. We'd all better get inside."

In the tiny Sunday School classroom where
Kathy's mother taught, Alfred whispered to D.J.
"That new kid sure dresses up for these mountains!
That suit looks expensive."

D.J. glanced at the kid, and then out the small
window without answering. Suddenly, he stiffened.

Alfred straightened up to follow his friend's eyes.
"What's the matter, D.J.?"

"The brindle!" he whispered. "I just saw it!"

Mrs. Stagg spoke firmly. "D.J. and Alfred. Are you
ready to begin the lesson?"

Reluctantly, D.J. turned away from looking out
the window, faced the front of the room, and nodded. Alfred waited until the teacher finished her
opening prayer, then he leaned over to whisper.

"The brindle that attacked Hero?"

"Yes." D.J. was tense with excitement. "I only got
a glimpse of him, but I'm sure!"

"Was he alone?"

"Yes."

"What's he doing here in Stoney Ridge?"

Before D.J. could reply, Mrs. Stagg asked, "D.J.,
what do you think the answer is?"

The boy squirmed, totally unaware of what the
question had been. D.J. tried not to look at Mrs.
Stagg's blue-green eyes. She was a slender, pretty
woman with a dimpled right cheek and short bru-
nette hair. She smiled pleasantly.

"I asked, D.J., what you thought it must have
been like to have seen Jesus on Resurrection
morning?"

D.J. glanced at Alfred and shrugged. He wasn't
thinking about Easter.

"You know, D.J.," the lay pastor's wife said, her dimple showing more, "since you're going to be a writer someday, would you write something special about Easter? Perhaps a personal experience essay? Then read it to us next Sunday—Easter morning."

The class giggled, and the new kid, Thad, wore a gleeful grin. D.J. nodded without enthusiasm. "OK."

Mrs. Stagg thanked D.J. and continued with the lesson, but the boy couldn't concentrate. He kept stealing glances out the window in hopes of seeing the brindle again.

After church services, D.J. tried to persuade his father to drive around looking for the brindle, but Dad Dillon wouldn't. D.J. also tried to persuade his father to let him go interview the hermit that afternoon, but Dad Dillon was firm. No working on Sunday. The Milfords came over to visit, so D.J. had Alfred to talk with part of the afternoon.

"There's one good thing about seeing that brindle," D.J. told Alfred as they sat on the Dillon front porch after lunch.

"What's that?"

"Since the pit bull was in town, that means the long-haired man and boy with the other two dogs probably were close by."

"That's true," Alfred agreed.

"That's also dangerous, because we may run into them anywhere, even just out walking around."

"If we did, we could call the animal control officer and have the dogs picked up for attacking Hero."

"I'd rather find them myself," D.J. said firmly. "But right now, let's go call the vet and see how Hero's doing."

The veterinarian's feminine voice said, "There's no change."

"Do — do you think he's going to make it?"

"Let's hope so! But we won't know until about Tuesday afternoon — if there's no infection. Meantime, I've done all I can; it's up to nature."

And God, D.J. thought as he hung up the phone. Then he wasn't quite sure how important a dog was to God. Still, if Hero meant so much to D.J., then probably God cared about Hero too.

D.J. slept a little better that night. He awakened at first light, dressed, and told his parents good-bye. He took the tape recorder, his note pad, and pencils downtown to meet Alfred. D.J. kept his eyes open for sign of the brindle, but there was nothing moving except the deliverymen at the town's small grocery store.

Alfred hadn't seen anything either, so the boys walked into the mountains and down into the canyon toward Mad River. They spotted the old hermit's one-room shack and started down the narrow trail toward it.

D.J. glanced ahead. He looked vainly for the old man by the small woodshed, then a tumbling-down garage-like building where he kept a few hand tools, and on to a windmill that had long ago collapsed.

"We should've heard his old dog barking by now," Alfred said.

"Maybe the dog can't hear us. I remember Mr. Zeering said Tug's old and toothless and almost blind. He probably can't hear too well either."

As the boys got closer to the rickety shanty* nestled under a stand of incense cedar and ponderosa pines,* D.J. half expected to see Zeke Zeering come out on the split-log front porch. The boy could clearly remember when he and his father had first come up to the shack at dusk a long time ago. The old man had come out with a coal oil lantern.

Suddenly, D.J. stopped dead still. "Listen!"

Alfred cocked his head. "Sounds like somebody crying!"

"Couldn't be Mr. Zeering," D.J. said softly. "What would he have to cry about?"

The boys traced the sound around the corner of the rough-hewn lumber that made up the little home. The hermit's back was to the boys. Zeke Zeering was crouched under a small young cedar with wide-spreading branches that swept gracefully to the ground.

D.J. saw the man wore threadbare, brown-striped railroad overalls, a patched blue workshirt, and a sweat-stained fedora.*

"Mr. Zeering?" D.J. called softly, hearing the sobbing sounds.

Slowly, the old hermit turned around and rose. He held a short-handled shovel. He was of medium height, well along in years, with a grizzled face that showed he hadn't shaved in many a day. He probably hadn't taken a bath for longer, D.J. realized.

There were tearstains down the hermit's cheeks. He spoke with a broken voice. "They done killed my dog!"

For the first time, D.J. saw the freshly-covered grave under the deep shade of the young cedar tree.

"I'm sorry!" D.J. exclaimed, feeling so keenly the possible death of his own dog.

Alfred asked, "Who killed your dog?"

"Don't rightly know." The hermit's voice was low and filled with anguish. "I went a'fishin' at sunup, and ol' Tug come with me. But he got tired, I guess, and he come on home by hisself. I heard him a'fightin' with some other dogs, and some people's voices, so I come a'runnin', but it was too late."

D.J.'s heart nearly stopped. "Did you see them?"

The old man shook his head. "Just heard the voices; didn't see nobody 'cepting three dogs." He wiped his eyes on his left sleeve and waved the shovel toward the dense forest.

"Were there two big ones and a brindle-colored pit bull?" D.J. asked breathlessly.

The hermit's eyes blazed. "That's them! Tell me where you seen them and I'll take my double-barrel shotgun to the lot of them for killin' my poor ol' toothless hound!"

D.J. started to answer when a man's voice called from the deep shadows of the ponderosas beyond the clearing.

"Hello! Anybody home?"

The hermit yelled, "You comin' friendly?"

"Friendly," the voice called. "Sheriff's office. OK to come on in?"

"Come on in!" the hermit called. He dropped his shovel and rubbed his hands on his coveralls. "Now boys, what in thunder would the law be a'doin' out here? Recken they already know about my dog bein' killed?"

D.J. saw a uniformed deputy come carefully forward, followed by a plainclothesman. They stopped well back from the old man and the boys.

"I'm Deputy Carlin," the uniformed officer said. "This is Detective Sergeant Padoffski. You're Zeke Zeering?"

"Shore am! What kin I do fer you fellers?"

"Who are these boys?" the plainclothesman asked.

"I'm D.J. Dillon. This is Alfred Milford."

"Are you Caleb Dillon's grandson?" the uniform deputy asked.

D.J. nodded. "Yes. Mr. Kersten, the newspaper editor, asked me to come interview Mr. Zeering. We just got here. A dog pack killed his hound." D.J. indicated the new grave.

"We're sorry," the detective sergeant said. "We'll send the animal control officer out to take your statement. Now, Mr. Zeering, is it OK with you if we look around?"

"Why, I recken so. But what you be lookin' fer?"

"Somebody threatened to blow up the new dam, and we're searching for some stolen dynamite."

The old hermit managed a weak smile. "Well, now, you won't find none of that hereabouts, so help yerselves to a look-see."

"Thanks," the two officers said together. They walked up on the rickety, old porch and entered the shack.

The hermit shook his head. "Boys, I wish they hadn't never built that dam. But I ain't the type that'd do it no harm neither, although I could if I wanted. See, I used to be a powder monkey.*"

D.J. asked, "What's a powder monkey?"

"That's what they used to call us men who handled the dynamite for blastin' back in the old days. I'd drill and tamp* the sticks in real good, light the

fuse, and run. I'd yell, 'Fire in the hole!' and
everybody'd take cover. Me too. Then there'd be
this awful boom! The whole mountain would jump
up and the ground would shake. But that was a
long time ago. . . ."

He let his voice trail off as the officers came out
of the door. The uniformed one was carrying a
stout wooden box with *Danger! Explosives* printed
on it in big letters.

The hermit exclaimed, "Now where in tarnation
did you fellers git that?"

The plainclothesman cleared his throat. "Mr.
Zeering, you're under arrest for suspicion of threatening to blow up the dam. You have the right to remain silent. . . ."

D.J. didn't hear the rest, but he knew the officer
was reading Mr. Zeering his rights. When that was
completed, he handcuffed the old man's hands behind his back.

D.J. had watched in stunned silence. Now he
protested. "There's got to be some mistake! Mr.
Zeering wouldn't do anything like that! Why, once
he saved my dog's life —"

The uniformed officer interrupted. "You may get
a chance to tell it to the judge. Now, you boys better
get on home."

The hermit had seemed so surprised; he hadn't
said anything since being arrested. Now he cried,
"Lookee here, Mr. Lawman! I don't know where
that dynamite come from, nor nothing about no
threat to no dam! You got the *wrong* man!"

"That's what they all say!" the plainclothes officer
answered wearily. "Well, let's get out of here so we

can book you into the county jail. You boys better get moving toward home!"

The hermit turned bloodshot eyes toward D.J. "I remember you and your little dog! Dillon, is it?"

"D.J. Dillon, yes."

"Well, now I can't rightly say I got me a friend in this whole world 'ceptin' you. Fact is, I ain't got nothing 'cept trouble this day. You goin' to stay my friend or you all a'goin' to cut and run even though these lawmen done got the wrong man?"

D.J. glanced at Alfred, then at the hermit. "You got two friends, Mr. Zeering. We'll stand with you."

"Thankee kindly, boys. Now would you all mind finishin' ol' Tug's grave for me? I'd be much obliged."

"We'll finish," D.J. said softly. "Now don't you worry! We believe you're innocent, and we'll help you prove it!"

As soon as the three men turned toward the trail into the ponderosas, Alfred demanded, "What'd you say that for, D.J.?"

"I don't know." He picked up the shovel. "But I gave my word."

Alfred groaned. "As if you didn't have enough troubles already!"

After the boys finished their sad task, they stood silently looking down at the fresh mound of dirt under the cedar. D.J. hoped Hero wouldn't also have to be buried soon.

As they left the hermit's place, Alfred asked, "Do you think kids our age can visit Mr. Zeering in jail? You've still got to interview him for the newspaper."

D.J. had forgotten all about the assignment. "I guess we'll have to call and find out."

The friends climbed out of the river canyon and entered an open meadow with a few scattered conifers.* A small stand of evergreens grew straight ahead of the boys at the meadow's end. On the right, the meadow slanted steeply upward toward a mountain called Lookout Peak. There was a cross at the top where Easter sunrise services were held each year. To the boys' left, the meadow ended at a canyon rim above the river.

D.J. said, "You know, if Mr. Zeering really is innocent, and somebody is framing him, then they're liable to come after us for getting involved."

"We're just helping a man who once saved your dog's life."

"Maybe whoever framed him doesn't know that, or care. Until Saturday, we never saw that bearded man or his kid before, or their dogs. So they're strangers. Hmm? What were they doing at the hermit's this morning. Maybe hiding the dynamite the deputies found?"

"What?" Alfred cried.

"Don't you see? It's logical! Tug came home and surprised those two and their three dogs. But they all ran off into the woods so Mr. Zeering never saw anyone; just the dogs! So maybe they haven't gone very far!"

As if in confirmation, two big dogs' deep voices sounded from the stand of timber at the meadow's edge. A smaller dog answered from straight ahead.

Alfred exclaimed, "That's them! What'll we do—run?"

"No! We can't outrun them! Climb one of these trees. Those dogs are closing in fast!"

Chapter Four

A MEAN DOG NAMED BOOG

In a few minutes, D.J. clung to the trunk of a young ponderosa pine and peered down fifteen feet at two big dogs barking furiously below him. A third dog, the smaller pit bull, ran around a nearby Douglas fir with a deadly, silent purpose. D.J. could see Alfred safely perched there about twenty feet up.

Alfred called, "They're the same dogs that jumped Hero in town!"

"Sure are!" D.J. agreed.

He studied the pit bull as he stopped circling Alfred's tree. The small, heavily-muscled dog placed his forefeet on the trunk and stretched his muzzle upward toward Alfred. The pit bull still did not bark. D.J. wasn't usually afraid of any dog, but there was something scary about the brindle's silent, purposeful movements.

D.J.'s eyes flickered back to the two bigger dogs below. They were barking furiously and leaping

high against the tree trunk. They ripped chunks of
bark off with their powerful jaws before falling
back to the brown pine needles that carpeted the
forest floor.

"Well!" A man's voice came from the forest shadows. "Rulon, look what our dogs done treed for us!"

D.J. saw the bearded, long-haired man who'd
bumped into him in town. A heavy rifle was cradled
in the crook of his right arm. The equally long-
haired boy called Rulon moved into a shaft of sun-
light. He carried a smaller .22 caliber rifle.

"Kinda spindly and puny, Pa," Rulon said with a
short laugh. "I'd rather have me a good 'possum up
there than that kind of human polecat."

D.J. held onto the tree limb with his right hand
and cupped his left one to his mouth. "How about
calling off your dogs, Mister?"

The man shouted at the dogs. "Ranger! Trig! Shut
up! Quiet, I say!"

Reluctantly, the animals stopped barking and
jumping. They tucked their tails between their legs
and slunk off into the shadows. D.J. had a hunch
Hero wasn't the only dog that the man's boots had
kicked.

D.J. watched as Rulon called to the brindle.
"Boog! Come here!"

The brindle didn't pay any attention. He continued to stare silently into Alfred's tree.

"I said, 'Come here!' " Rulon repeated, running
toward the powerfully built dog.

Instantly, the brindle spun about and silently
faced the long-haired boy. Rulon stopped short in
his tracks. D.J. saw the brindle's hackles* stand up

on his neck. The lip curled back from his long fangs, but the dog did not bark or growl.

"Careful, Rulon!" the father called. "You know that ornery cuss won't mind nobody but me! Boog, come here!"

The brindle's hackles relaxed. Slowly, still watching the boy, the brindle moved toward the man. Rulon's father snapped a stout chain to the dog's wide leather collar.

D.J. sighed. "Thanks, Mister!" He started climbing down from the tree, aware that Alfred was also easing down to the ground from his perch.

D.J.'s heart raced as he watched the man chain the pit bull to the stout, thick roots of an uprooted black oak. D.J. brushed off his clothes and thought quickly. He had found the people and the dogs who had hurt Hero. One was named Rulon. Now what?

D.J. turned to check the other dogs. The big mastiff cross called Trig was sitting on his haunches by a stump. The German shepherd called Ranger had flopped down into the brown pine needles.

The man demanded, "Who're you kids?"

"I'm D.J. Dillon. He's Alfred Milford." D.J. paused, but when the man only grunted, D.J. asked, "Who're you?"

"Beau Krockner," the bearded man replied.

The long-haired boy snorted. "Beauregard, but you'd better not call him that if you know what's good for you!"

"Shut up!" the man snapped to the boy, then added to D.J. and Alfred, "That loudmouth's my boy, Rulon." The man suddenly bent his head slightly forward to stare at D.J. and Alfred. "Hey!

Ain't we'uns met before somewheres?"

D.J. nodded. "We bumped into each other in Indian Springs a couple days ago."

"Yeah? Oh, yeah! You ran into us when Rulon and me was a'chasin' our dogs! They'd been in a fight with some strange mutt!"

Alfred exclaimed, "That was D.J.'s dog! Your pack nearly killed him!"

"Yeah?" the man shifted the heavy rifle slightly. "Well, dogs will fight, ya know."

D.J. thought of Hero maybe dying right now, and the boy's anger flared. "Hero wouldn't fight unless he had to! He was tied up on a short leash! He couldn't get away, and he couldn't even defend himself!"

The long-haired kid laughed scornfully. "Now, ain't that just too bad?"

D.J. felt a rush of anger sweep over him. He raised his voice. "I want you to pay my dog's vet bills! And your dogs should be on leashes when they're in town! That's the law!"

Beau Krockner raised a hand from the heavy rifle. "Easy, now—D.J. I'm plumb sorry your dog got hurt, but *nobody* tells me what to do! That includes the law! This here's my law!" He patted the stock of the heavy rifle.

D.J. swallowed hard at the implied threat. Still, he was mad. It was hard to control such anger and frustration.

Alfred helped. He laid a warning hand on D.J.'s stiffening shoulders and whispered, "Easy, D.J.! Don't say anything more!"

Beau nodded. "Your friend talks sense! Now, me'n my boy are a'goin' to walk out of here with our dogs. You forget you saw us, ya hear?"

D.J. glared, too upset to trust his voice.

Rulon added a warning. "You don't, and we'll sic Boog on you! You might drive them other two off if you cussed and kicked loud and long enough, but not this here brindle!"

"Shut up, Rulon!" Beau yelled. His tone made the two big dogs jump. They tucked their tails between their legs and slunk low to the ground. But Boog continued to stare silently at D.J. and Alfred.

Father and son unsnapped the brindle's chain and started to walk away, but D.J. called after them.

"Mr. Krockner, I can't just let you get away with it!"

The man turned around to face D.J. and laughed, low and mean. "Now, sonny boy, anytime you think you can stop me, you just go right ahead and try! I won't have to lift a finger because Boog will take care of you—and your four-eyed friend!"

The long-haired pair walked off into the dense shadows with their dogs. D.J. was so upset he was trembling as he stepped away from the tree.

"It's not right, Alfred! It's not fair! They hurt my dog—maybe killed him! I just can't let them get away scot-free!"

"Well, there's nothing we can do now! So relax and let's get to a phone."

Back in Stoney Ridge, D.J. used the pay phone outside of the local mercantile store to call the veterinary hospital in Indian Springs. After the call D.J. looked at Alfred through sad eyes.

"No change. The vet says there's nothing anybody can do but wait until about tomorrow afternoon when the danger should be past."

Alfred laid a hand gently on D.J.'s shoulder. "It'll be OK! Come on! Let's go to the sheriff's substation and see if we can talk to the animal control officer about the Krockners and their dogs!"

The boys turned away from the pay telephone. D.J. said evenly, "If the county doesn't do something right away about those dogs—especially that brindle—I'm going to!"

"Like what?"

"I don't know yet! In fact, I should do something whether Hero gets well or not!"

Alfred frowned. "You're talking strangely! Revenge isn't—"

"And I will too!" D.J. interrupted. "I'm going to do something, no matter what!"

Chapter Five

THE NEWSPAPER EDITOR'S SURPRISE

As the boys approached the city park with the sheriff's substation at the far end, D.J. said, "Don't let me forget to find out if they'll let us visit Mr. Zeering in jail. Maybe we can help him prove he didn't plan to dynamite the dam."

"You're sure he's innocent?"

"I'm positive. He's different, but I'm sure he'd never blow up a dam."

"I don't know, D.J. Just because he found Hero when he was hurt and nursed him back to health doesn't necessarily mean. . . ."

The sentence was left unfinished as Thad Thorkell came out the front door of the sheriff's substation. Thad wore clean blue jeans and a light yellow windbreaker. He stopped and waited for D.J. and Alfred to start up the steps.

"Hi!" Thad called. "What brings you two here?"

D.J. answered, "We could ask you the same thing."

"I was just telling the deputy that my father and I are planning to demonstrate against the dam, but it will be peaceful." He abruptly changed the subject. "Say, where's Kathy?"

D.J. shrugged. "We haven't seen her today."

"If you do," Thad replied, "tell her she's welcome to join the demonstration. You guys can come too, if you want."

"Thanks," D.J. said without enthusiasm.

Thad hurried across the city park.

Alfred said, "He sure seems to think a lot of Kathy."

D.J. growled, "You know what, Alfred? Thad could be the bomber!"

"Now, D.J., I thought you suspected Beau and Rulon. Besides, Thad's not old enough to handle dynamite."

"His father is! I wouldn't put it past them to have planted those explosives at Mr. Zeering's place so he'd get blamed!"

"Aw, D.J., they probably don't even know where the hermit lives. You're just upset with everybody because of Hero's condition."

"No, Alfred, there's something about those Thorkells I don't like. I can't explain it, but I felt that way the moment I saw them."

"But they dress well and go to church—"

D.J. interrupted. "Yeah, but what was it we memorized recently about the 'false prophets' that Paul the Apostle mentioned?" (2 Corinthians 11:13)

"D.J., I'm surprised at you! You're really looking for far-out things!"

D.J. felt a momentary annoyance over his friend's

candor. Then D.J. took a deep breath and nodded. "Maybe you're right. Boy! I sure hope the Lord isn't as upset with me as I am with everybody—including myself!"

"I can understand how you feel. After all, life isn't very fair sometimes."

"It sure isn't!"

"Hey, I know what let's do!" Alfred cried, slapping his hand on D.J.'s back.

"What?"

"We could visit the dam, or at least the town of Yellow Dog."

"Why should we do that?"

"You could interview some people there on how they feel about the dam and their town going to be under a hundred feet of water. Mr. Kersten would like that. He likes human interest stuff, you know. Maybe he'd even give you some extra money to help pay your vet bill!"

D.J. started to shake his head, but Alfred plunged on. "You promised your folks you'd let the sheriff's department handle those people and their dogs. So let's just give the deputies the Krockners' names and let them take care of everything. What d'ya say?"

"I don't know, Alfred. I'm so mad at what they did to Hero, I want to do something to them myself!"

"What was it Mrs. Stagg said in Sunday School a week or so ago about the Bible saying, 'Be ye angry, and sin not'? (Ephesians 4:26) Remember?"

"I remember. I'm so upset! Oh, well—if the deputies will do something. . . ."

He let his voice trail off as he pushed open the

front door to the small sheriff's substation. Through
the opening in a glass partition, D.J. told the lone
uniformed woman officer that he'd found out the
names of the people whose dogs had attacked
Hero. D.J. didn't know where they lived.

The woman deputy was sympathetic but not very
helpful. "That's the animal control officer's responsibility, but he's still in the eastern end of the county. I can take your number and have him contact
you the next time he's back in the office."

D.J. felt his insides churn with frustration. "Then
can I see a man who was jailed? Mr. Zeering was
arrested on suspicion of making a bomb threat."

"Sorry, boys, but minors aren't allowed to visit
prisoners."

D.J. was really feeling steamed up when he and
Alfred walked outside. D.J. cried, "See? I can't get
in to see the hermit, so I can't interview him! That
means I can't get paid for the story, so I've go no
money to repay Brother Paul—plus whatever else
I'll owe the vet!"

"Now, D.J.—"

D.J. broke in, waving his arms. "Nothing's being
done about the Krockners and their dogs either!
They could skip the county without anything ever
being done to them!"

Alfred spoke quietly and said, "When you calm
down, would you think about going to Yellow Dog
and the dam site?"

"Yeah, we should check things out in both
places. But it's too late today. It'll be dark soon,"
D.J. replied. The boys agreed to meet early the next
morning for the walk to the dam site.

Two Mom greeted D.J. as he came in about dusk. She was seated at the kitchen table clipping coupons from magazines. She saved a few cents on many items by trading in the coupons at the supermarket in Indian Springs.

She looked up and greeted her stepson. "Mr. Kersten phoned just a minute ago. He wants you to call him at home right away, please."

The thought of what Mr. Kersten would say because D.J. hadn't interviewed Zeke Zeering made the boy nervous. But when the editor came on the line, his voice was cheerful.

"Oh, D.J.! Thanks for calling me back. I need to fill you in on the bomb threat you asked me about on the phone. Well, now that the dam's close to completion, someone has threatened to dynamite it. I guess you know about your friend the hermit being arrested as a suspect in that threat?"

The boy sighed with relief that the editor wasn't angry with him. "Yes, I—"

Mr. Kersten interrupted. "Well, obviously you didn't have time to get that interview before now. But he's out, so you can—"

D.J. exclaimed, "He's out of jail?"

"Yes! Now, you get down to his shack—"

D.J. couldn't help interrupting. He remembered a term he'd heard around the newspaper and sheriff's office when he was doing his job as a stringer.

"You mean they let him out on his own rec— recog—"

"Own recognizance?* Oh, no! There's no way they'd let someone out on his O.R. after being charged with making a bomb threat. Mr. Zeering made bail."

"Bail?"

"Yeah! Somebody put up money to guarantee that the hermit will return for a hearing at an appointed time."

"But I didn't think Mr. Zeering had a dime to his name."

"Probably doesn't, D.J. Someone probably posted the money for him."

"Who would do that?"

"I don't know. Why?"

"Well," the boy said slowly into the receiver, "Alfred and I were there when Mr. Zeering was arrested, and he told us he didn't have a friend in the world. So who would have posted bail? And why would anyone want to get him out of jail?"

"Ask him when you see him. Find him and try to get that interview before Tuesday afternoon!"

D.J. sighed. "Yes, Mr. Kersten."

"Oh, one thing more. Please be careful. I know the hermit likes you, but don't upset him any more than he is already."

"He won't hurt me."

"Well, he might hurt somebody. I talked to the jailer today. He told me that the hermit nearly went crazy being locked up."

D.J. nodded. He could understand how a man who lived in the mountains would hate a tiny jail cell.

The editor continued, "From what I heard, the hermit is mad at the world. He's already got the reputation of being an ornery old cuss, living by himself all those years. But he was really mad today. Swore he would never again be locked up."

D.J. felt a sense of concern for the old man. "He just wants to be left alone out there in the woods."

"Probably so. But the deputy told me the hermit threatened that the sheriff's office had better not ever come for him again.

"So, D.J., maybe he is mad enough to try blowing up the dam! He's got the experience to do it. He used to be a powder monkey, I heard."

The boy nodded. "I know. But I think he's innocent. I think somebody's trying to frame him."

"Frame him? Why?"

"I don't know, but I think he's a nice old guy— not mean and nasty like people say. Why, if it hadn't been for him, my dog would have died when Ol' Satchelfoot—"

The editor interrupted again. "I've got a call coming in on the other line. I need that interview but I don't want you to take any foolish chances. Call me after you talk to the hermit, and I'll help you write the story. Your byline, of course, and your money. 'Bye, now."

D.J. hung up, frowning in deep thought. Two Mom looked up from where she had finished clipping the coupons at the kitchen table. "Something wrong, D.J.?"

He told her what the editor had said.

Two Mom stacked the clipped magazines neatly on the table and carried the coupons to a drawer under the drainboard. "Maybe Mr. Zeering has friends he doesn't know about."

D.J. shook his head so the unruly blond hair flipped back and forth across his forehead. "I don't think so."

"Then what else could it be?"

D.J. leaned against the refrigerator, thinking. Suddenly, a thought hit him. It was so wild D.J. pushed himself away from the refrigerator so hard it rocked.

"D.J.! What on earth...?"

"Two Mom, what if somebody was really going to blow up the dam — and Mr. Zeering was blamed? He's already been put in jail on suspicion. I mean, the officers found that dynamite on his place and all."

Two Mom smiled patiently. "D.J., why would someone want to get Mr. Zeering blamed for something like that? I think your imagination has blown this whole thing into something it's not."

"What else could it be?" he demanded.

"Well, I don't know, but I'm sure it's not—"

D.J. broke in. "Just the same, I've got to tell Mr. Zeering what I think."

"Not tonight! It would be dark before you could get up to his shack and back."

"I could take a flashlight."

"Into that river canyon? I'm sorry, but no!" Two Mom pulled a yellow flowered apron from the middle drawer under the drainboard. "Now, you'd better work on that report Mrs. Stagg asked you to write about Easter."

Reluctantly, D.J. started for his bedroom, but a sense of urgency and excitement gripped him. *What if somebody really is planning to blow up the dam and frame the hermit? And if he resists going back to jail, he will really look guilty. Boy! I've got to talk to him the first thing tomorrow morning. I hope it's not too late!*

Chapter Six

A NEW DANGER

D.J. awoke at dawn. He was to meet Alfred this morning for a tour of Yellow Dog, but first D.J. had to see Zeke Zeering. D.J. pulled his robe over his pajamas and padded rapidly down the hallway in slippers that slapped softly on the carpet.

Dad Dillon came out of the bathroom, wiping his wet hands on a small towel. He was fully dressed except for his boots. He had them on, but they weren't laced.

"Oh, D.J.—Brother Paul called last night after you were asleep. He's shorthanded on men to help repair the cross on Lookout Peak for the sunrise services. I told him I'd ask you to come along and help."

"Aw, Dad! I've got things to do today!"

"Something more important than helping out the preacher at Easter?"

The boy hesitated, thinking fast. He didn't have to visit Yellow Dog. But he *did* have to see the hermit.

"No. But Dad, first I've got to see the hermit."

"Two Mom told me about your idea of someone trying to frame that old hermit. I agree with her — your imagination is running away with you."

"It wouldn't hurt to tell Mr. Zeering what I suspect, would it, Dad?"

"No, I guess not. But we could use you today to help set up for Sunday. John Milford's bringing Alfred, so you two could work together."

D.J. nodded. That meant Alfred already knew they couldn't go to Yellow Dog this morning. It wouldn't be so bad helping repair the cross if his best friend were there. Still, D.J. held off. "Could I first tape an interview with Mr. Zeering? The editor needs that today for sure, and I need the money for Hero's vet bill."

"I suppose you could do that first. Then take a shortcut up the side of Lookout Peak and meet us there. Fair enough?"

"Fair enough!" The boy almost sighed with relief, then thought of something else. "Then could you drive me into Indian Springs to deliver the tape and let me see my dog?"

"Haven't you been phoning the vet?"

"Yes, but today's the danger point. I thought Hero might feel better if he could see me. I'd certainly feel better if I could see him too."

Dad threw the towel over his shoulder. "OK, I guess."

* * * * *

When D.J. reached the hermit's cabin, the boy was surprised how much the old man had changed since D.J. had last seen him. Mr. Zeering's watery blue eyes were bloodshot and sort of wild-looking. He was of medium height, yet his shoulders were now bent, making him look smaller.

His striped railroad coveralls seemed more threadbare than D.J. remembered. The old man's clothes had been washed, and he'd shaved and probably taken a shower.

Mr. Zeering paced back and forth on the rickety, split-log front porch of the shack he had built many years ago. The restless movements reminded D.J. of caged animals he had seen in a zoo.

Right away, D.J. told the hermit about the editor wanting a taped interview. But the hermit wasn't in a mood for that. So D.J. told the hermit his suspicions about someone maybe wanting Mr. Zeering released from jail so he could be blamed for something terrible. "Like maybe if the dam was blown up," D.J. concluded.

The old man didn't seem to hear. He didn't even answer the boy. Instead, it seemed the hermit's mind was somewhere else. His bloodshot eyes skimmed the beauty of the surrounding trees and mountains.

"D.J., I ain't never a'goin' back to any jail! Never! Why, I like to of died in that tiny cell! And I never done *nothing* to nobody! So why would somebody do *this* to me?"

The boy felt that way about Hero and the Krockners, but D.J. didn't say anything. He removed the light-blue windbreaker he was wearing and spread it over the top of an old stump that had been sawed off near the hermit's rickety front porch. The boy sat on the stump, feeling the fresh spring breeze caressing his face.

He couldn't stand to look at the terrible sadness in the hermit's leathery, lined face. D.J. turned his eyes toward the young incense cedar* and the fresh grave where Tug lay buried. The boy tried not to think that soon he might have to bury Hero.

Well, I tried to tell him, D.J. told himself. He reached down to the daypack he'd placed against the stump. "Mr. Zeering, I've just got to interview you for the newspaper. I need the money to pay my dog's vet bill." The boy removed a small, battery-operated tape recorder from his pack.

The hermit didn't seem to hear him. He paused in his pacing to look straight at the boy. "D.J., if it hadn't a'been for that there lawyer feller, I'd still be locked up! Only not for long. I'd a'either found a way to escape, or I'd a'died!"

"Lawyer?"

"Never set eyes on him before, but he got me out. Said he was representing a client who was making my bail."

"Oh?" D.J. felt his excitement rising again. "Who was his client?"

"Lawyer feller told me he couldn't say. Something about a client-attorney relationship and privileged information. But I don't care! I'm free, D.J., and I ain't never a'goin' back to jail!"

The boy hesitated. "Mr. Zeering, I don't know much about the law, but doesn't bail just mean you're out on a promise to come back later for a hearing or something?"

"Yep! That's what the lawyer feller done told me! But I ain't a'goin' back! They might try to put me back in that there jailhouse—but I *won't go!*"

D.J. checked the recorder to make sure it was ready to operate. "But doesn't that mean the person who put up your bail money will lose it? And the sheriff will come after you for jumping bail, and—"

"Put me back in jail? No, siree! I won't let 'em take me back there! Never!" Mr. Zeering's eyes blazed and he waved his hands as he spoke, then turned them into fists. He shook them in the direction the sheriff's officers had come for him a few days before.

D.J. swallowed a little uneasily. He had never seen the hermit so agitated. The man's pacing increased, causing the weathered front porch to squeak like a small, frightened animal.

"What—what'll you do?" the boy asked softly. He wondered if the old man owned a gun.

The hermit stopped pacing. He looked at D.J. with eyes that suddenly seemed cold and hard. "Cain't rightly tell ye that, D.J. But they'll be sorry— they'll *all* be sorry they ever come out here a'bothering me for somethin' I never done!"

It took some time before the old man settled down. D.J. convinced the hermit to start from the beginning and tell his story into the recorder. At first, Mr. Zeering watched the recorder suspiciously, as if it might jump up and bite him. But as he continued talking, the hermit forgot the recorder. He talked faster and faster, his voice rising.

He told about growing up in the Carolinas; of caring for a pretty young woman who never cared for him. She married someone else. Mr. Zeering said he then became a drifter, going off by himself for longer and longer periods. "Got me neither chick nor kin," he said, stopping for a moment.

Then he resumed talking. He told about how he learned to work with dynamite. When he needed money, he'd work for a while as a powder monkey.

"I kept on a'drifting, I recken, maybe fifteen, twenty years. Finally, I found this spot and built on it. Nobody never come here in them days. Wild, it was, and peaceful. Then that changed. Building the dam changed things most. They're a'killin' the trees and the hills themselves. And they're a'killin' me."

The hermit stepped stiffly off the porch and walked toward a nearby ponderosa. D.J. picked up the tape recorder and followed, trying not to lose any of the old man's words.

"Them engineer fellers made a mark on this here tree. See it?"

Mr. Zeering pointed above his head to a small notch in the tree's bark. "Told me the water would rise clean up to there! Drown my house! Drown my dog's grave! Drown me too, fer all I care!"

D.J. didn't say anything. He followed the hermit back to the porch. They sat down together on the top step, the recorder between them.

"Lived here a powerful long time, I have." The old man's eyes took on a soft, faraway look. He didn't seem to see the beautiful trees and mountains anymore.

D.J. waited silently, not sure what to say. Finally, the hermit spoke. "For years, nothing changed here. It was wilderness. But when they started building the dam, it brought in people and machines and noise. Then them dogs killed my poor, old, toothless, practically blind Tug. He never done nothing to hurt nobody. Me neither! So why'd they do that to us?"

Mr. Zeering looked toward the dog's grave. A tear ran down the wrinkled cheek. D.J. swallowed hard and looked away. He hurt for the old man.

D.J. reached over and pushed the recorder's stop button. "Thanks, Mr. Zeering," he said, rising from where he'd been sitting on the top porch step. "My editor will like that."

"Write me up a good story, D.J. Tell 'em the truth, jist like I done told you. That's all I ask."

"I will," D.J. promised. "Well, I've got to go help my dad. He and some men are repairing the cross on Lookout Peak for Easter sunrise services."

The hermit plucked a splinter from the slender post that supported the porch's sagging roof. "Easter." He said the word softly. "Ain't thought of that in a coon's age,* I recken. But I see that there cross on top of the mountain, and I think about it sometimes."

D.J. removed the tape from the machine but stopped before putting it in his pack. He glanced at the hermit, surprised at the man's words.

"You ever been to church, Mr. Zeering?"

The old man rolled the splinter between his lips before answering. "Yep! Once, when I was about your age, I hit the sawdust trail.* Went to church reg'lar. That's where I met that purty gal I told you about. But when she wouldn't have none of me, I got mad at her—and God. Ain't been in a church since."

D.J. had never heard such sadness in a man's voice. The boy said a little uncertainly, "You could come to the sunrise services with me if you want."

D.J. wasn't sure how people at church would react to Mr. Zeering. Still, Brother Paul always said
every soul was precious to the Lord. "You could sit
with me," D.J. added hopefully.

Mr. Zeering shook his head. The untidy locks of
his gray hair were caught in a little gust of wind.
"Thankee kindly, D.J., but I dassn't."

"You don't dare? Why not?" D.J. asked, feeling a
growing concern for this strange old man.

"Well, for one thing, it's dangerous."

"Going to church?"

"No, getting there." The hermit pointed. "I'm
down in this canyon by the river. But see up yonder
on the side of that mountain?"

To the west and downstream from the recluse's
cabin, there was an opening in the canyon that per-
mitted clear visibility of Lookout Peak. It rose ma-
jestically above the steep walls of Mad River and
the beautiful little area where the hermit lived.

D.J. looked up. "Where the cross is?"

"Underneath it, on the southeast side of Lookout
Peak. Ain't you never noticed what all that digging
for the dam has done to the ground up there?"

D.J. shook his head.

"Look closer, Boy! There's a whole mountain of
dirt up there just a'waitin' to let go and slide down."

D.J.'s eyes followed the old man's pointing hand.
"You mean an avalanche?"

"Much more than that! Look about a third of the
way up the side of that mountain. There's acres
and acres of dirt just a'waitin' for some hard rain!
When the rain comes, that whole mountainside will

let go and slide down. Wouldn't want to be downstream of it when it happens!"

D.J. glanced at the sky. Dark, threatening clouds
were drifting silently in from the southeast. D.J. could
see the scars where the great pieces of equipment
had gouged and scraped tons of earth from the
mountain for use at the dam farther downriver. But
the boy couldn't see how the mountainside might
be hit by the threatening storm. He started to say
so, but the old hermit read his mind.

"Always rains on Easter hereabouts. If enough of
it comes 'afore Sunday, it'll turn that whole mountainside to mud. It'll slide right down into them little meadows—you must've seen 'em—then slip
right into the canyon beside the river. It'll be the
biggest wall of mud in all creation."

"Mud?"

"Sure thing! Bury everything in front of it!"

"How do you know that for sure?"

The hermit snorted. "You don't spend years
blowing up mountains with blasting powder
unless'n you know what's going to happen to the
dirt you tear loose!"

"Shouldn't you warn somebody?" D.J. asked anxiously, glancing toward the possible slide.

The old man shrugged. He pointed out that he
lived well upstream from where the threatening
mountain stood. The natural slope of the higher
land would carry any slide into the canyon a half-
mile or more below his cabin. There the canyon was
so wide a landslide would probably not even reach
Mad River, but only fill the wide area scoured out of
the mountain over long centuries of erosion.

"Besides, ain't nothing in that canyon where the mud slide will go! No people or houses or nothing—just them little meadows and a stand of timber. Mud will likely end up in the canyon by the river. No harm done, 'less'n some fool's caught out there. Like me, if I was to risk a'goin' to them sunrise services if it's been raining hard."

Mr. Zeering paused and rubbed his watery eyes with the back of a withered hand. "Besides, who'd listen to me if I told them the danger? Everybody thinks I'm a mean, ornery old geezer who's tetched in the head.*"

"I don't think that, Mr. Zeering."

For a moment, the old man gazed silently at the boy. D.J. saw tears form in the red-rimmed eyes.

"You'd best be going to help yore pa and them others, D.J." The hermit turned and walked quickly into the shack. He didn't look back, not even when he closed the splintery door.

D.J. had a strange sense of uneasiness. Maybe it was hearing the sad story of the old hermit's life. Maybe it was knowing Hero was still fighting to stay alive. Maybe it was the knowledge that D.J. had to do something about Beau and Rulon's dangerous dogs.

Whatever it was, D.J. didn't like it. He tried to shake off the feeling. When the recorder was safe in his pack, D.J. hoisted it to his shoulders and started off.

As he passed the sagging woodshed, D.J. saw something glistening where the sun's rays penetrated a small mountain misery* plant. He bent and picked up a metallic button.

H-m-m-m. This isn't mine or Alfred's. Maybe one

of the deputies lost it the other day.

D.J. rubbed the button between his fingers as he began his climb out of the river canyon. He started across the first small meadow, and without think-ing, dropped the button inside his windbreaker pocket. D.J.'s eyes probed up to the acres of dirt clinging to the side of the mountain. *Looks safe to me,* he told himself. *But, I'd sure hate to be in the way if that ever does let go.*

Suddenly the sky was filled with the dark, rapid-ly-moving clouds D.J. had noticed earlier.

Wonder if the hermit's right? It does always seem to rain at Easter.

KATHY MEETS THE BRINDLE

The fast-moving clouds and the hint of rain made D.J. uneasy as he followed a deer trail up the side of the dangerous mountain. He sighed with relief when he reached the top of Lookout Peak. Boulders had been placed at the edge of the parking lot to keep cars from dropping over the edge of the Peak into the canyon.

As D.J. puffed into sight, he saw Brother Paul Stagg, Dad Dillon, Alfred's father, and another man from Stoney Ridge's only church. They had straightened the wooden cross at the very top of the mountain. The cross had been leaning dangerously because melting snows had washed away part of the foundation.

D.J. saw fresh cement had been poured into the hole at the foot of the cross. Alfred was washing out the small wheelbarrow where the wet cement had been mixed. The others watched Brother Paul, kneeling on an old coat and using a trowel to put some finishing touches on the cement base.

Dad Dillon frowned at his son. "We were expecting you long before this, D.J."

"Yeah, you missed all the fun," his best friend teased.

D.J. wanted to tell about his talk with the hermit and what he'd said about the possibility of a mud slide. But the big preacher spoke first.

"Now, Sam, recken D.J. got here as soon as he could." Brother Paul straightened up. Under his 10-gallon Stetson* hat, reddish-gold hair clung wetly to his temples.

D.J. explained, "It took me some time to get that interview taped with the hermit, Dad. I got here as quick as I could."

He changed the subject. "You know what? Mr. Zeering says the southeast side of this mountain is ready to let go and slide down into the canyon if it rains hard."

The men and Alfred walked over to the edge of the canyon and looked down.

"It looks OK to me," Alfred's father said.

"Me too," Dad agreed.

Brother Paul was more cautious. "Same here. Still, it wouldn't hurt to report it to the sheriff's office, just in case."

D.J. nodded. "I'll do that the next time I get a chance. Well, guess I'd better help clean up here."

He turned to help Alfred gather up the tools used in mixing the cement.

Alfred asked, "You ready to see Yellow Dog? I've never seen a town about to drown."

"I've got some things to do first," D.J. replied, helping load the wet wheelbarrow and tools into the back of a pickup. "Dad said he'd take me to Indian Springs to deliver the tape to Mr. Kersten.

"Then I'd like to go by the vet's and see my dog. He should be out of danger about now. I'd also like to find out if the animal control officer's done anything about the Krockners' dogs."

Brother Paul picked up an old gunnysack from the back of the pickup and briskly buffed the cement dust from his cowboy boots. His deep voice seemed to make the truck vibrate.

"No need for your father to make that trip, D.J. I'm taking Kathy into Indian Springs soon's I get cleaned up. She wants to buy something for her mother for Easter. You could ride with us."

"That'd be great, Brother Paul. You got room for Alfred if he wants to come along?"

"Sure thing!" the lay pastor rumbled. "Clear it with your fathers, and we'll be on our way."

A light rain had started falling when Brother Paul parked his old sedan at the veterinary hospital in Indian Springs. The lay pastor, his daughter, and Alfred entered the building with D.J. The smell of something used to control germs was unpleasant to the boy's nostrils.

The lady vet stood behind the counter, talking to the receptionist. Dr. Barner glanced up and greeted everyone.

"I was just going to call you, D.J." she said.

He leaned against the counter, his heart skipping a beat. "How's Hero doing?"

"Ordinarily, he'd be out of danger by now, but

he's developed a severe infection."

"Infection?" D.J. repeated, feeling his heart sink into his boots.

"There's a lot of bacteria involved in such wounds. We treated him with antibiotics as soon as you brought him in, but that hasn't been enough."

Kathy asked softly, her eyes wide, "Is he going to get well?"

"We're doing all we can, though sometimes those infections can be stubborn. But don't give up! Hero hasn't. He's a fighter! Most dogs would be dead by now if they'd been as badly hurt as he was. He can still make it!"

D.J. managed to control his voice so it wouldn't shake with the fear he felt. "Could I see him?"

"Yes, but only for a moment. The rest of you please wait here."

D.J.'s heart was beating so fast he could barely breath as the vet led the way down a long hallway and into a small room. Hero lay on a stainless steel table. The dog was so weak no restraints were used to keep him from falling off. Tubes protruded from various wounds.

D.J. had to try twice before he could make his voice heard by the still, silent form of his little dog.

"It's—it's me, Hero." D.J. spoke softly, his voice cracking. "I'm here, Boy!"

The dog did not move. D.J. tried again, slightly louder. "Hero, it's me—D.J." He reached out with a trembling hand and gently touched the dog's head between the torn ears. An unwelcome tear slid out of the corner of D.J.'s right eye and down his cheek.

He didn't want the vet to notice, so D.J. didn't

brush the tear away. He stood silently hurting while another tear dropped down his left cheek.

Dr. Barner touched D.J.'s shoulder and said, "Time to go, D.J."

The boy nodded. "I'm going, Hero. But I'll be back. You get well, OK?" He gave his dog a final gentle pat and started backing out of the room.

Then he stopped. Had Hero's stub tail moved slightly? D.J. glanced hopefully at Dr. Barner for confirmation, but she was heading out the door and couldn't have seen. "Hang on, Hero!" D.J. whispered. He followed the vet back down the hall toward the waiting room. There he stopped.

"You go on, please," D.J. whispered as they neared the end of the corridor. "I'll come in a minute. And—thanks."

"You're welcome, D.J." Dr. Barner did not turn around. She entered a side door. D.J. stood trembling, leaning against the hall wall. He didn't want his friends to see him until he had regained control of his emotions. He brushed both cheeks with his forefingers, blinked rapidly to clear his vision and walked into the waiting room. All eyes focused on him.

"I think he moved his tail when he heard my voice. Maybe he's getting better," D.J. said, trying to sound cheerful.

Kathy said softly, "I'm glad, D.J.! Real glad!"

Brother Paul stepped toward the outside door. "So far, so good. Let's get you to the sheriff's office next."

The sheriff's office was on the first floor of the old courthouse which perched on top of one of Indian Springs' seven steep hills. Brother Paul couldn't find a parking place. He dropped D.J. and

Alfred off by the wide front steps with instructions to meet them at a nearby coffee shop.

The friends entered the courthouse, climbed a few steps in an echoing hallway, and found themselves in a small office. Two uniformed women deputies were seated at desks. The older, heavier one listened to the boys' reasons for coming, then shook her head.

"The animal control officer is still in the far end of the county, near the Nevada border. He can't do anything about your complaint until he gets back, maybe tomorrow."

D.J. shook his head in frustration. *Nothing* was being done about the Krockners and their vicious dogs! D.J., still very upset over Hero's latest problem, turned away, then swung back.

"Oh, one thing more." He quickly told her about the possible mud slide on the side of Lookout Peak.

The woman officer said, "I'll make a note of it and pass the word along to the right people to check it out. But everyone's shorthanded, so it may be a while."

D.J. thanked her and walked beside Alfred down the long, echoing corridor.

"Alfred, I never wished anything bad for anybody or any animal—but it's not right for those people and their dogs to still be running loose! There must be something I can do!"

"It's not your place, D.J." Alfred said, pushing the heavy glass door open to the outside steps.

A cold wind had come up and the rain was falling harder. D.J. drew his windbreaker close about his shoulders and glanced at the threatening clouds.

"I'll make it my place! I'm not going to let them get away with it!"

Alfred lightly touched his friend's arm. "Brother Paul would probably say you've got a spiritual problem there. I mean, wanting revenge—"

"I don't want to hear about it!" D.J. snapped. He started hurrying down the street toward the coffee shop. "Come on! We've got to find Brother Paul and Kathy so I can deliver this tape to Mr. Kersten."

The newspaper editor wasn't in, so D.J. marked the tape label with a pen the receptionist loaned him. He left the tape and walked back out to the street.

Alfred stepped from behind a store window where he'd been to get away from the wind. "Brother Paul went into the men's store for a minute. Kathy's waiting—oh, no! Look! There's that environmentalist kid, Thad, talking with Kathy."

D.J.'s eyes followed his friend's pointing arm. Then he saw something else and stiffened.

Three dogs rounded the corner from an alley and trotted along down the street toward Kathy's back. D.J. recognized them at once: a German shepherd, a mastiff cross, and the brindled pit bull.

D.J.'s heart leaped into a full gallop as he tried to think what to do: call to Kathy or head for her? If the boys ran toward her, would the dogs consider it a challenge and attack?

Alfred whispered, "What should we do, D.J.?"

Before he could reply, Thad apparently said something funny. Kathy laughed and stepped back—right onto the left front paw of the passing pit bull!

Chapter Eight

CLUE IN A TOWN ABOUT TO DROWN

Instantly, the brindled pit bull swung his head toward the back of Kathy's leg. D.J. opened his mouth to yell to the unsuspecting girl. But it was too late. The brindle's powerful jaws snapped.

At the same time, Kathy glanced down to see what she'd stepped on. Instantly, she reacted. Thad hadn't moved.

D.J. saw the pit bull's teeth click harmlessly together. The dog looked up at Kathy. The slightly curved tail moved sideways in a tentative gesture of friendship. The other two dogs kept trotting.

D.J. and Alfred slowed as the bigger animals passed. Then the boys broke into a run through the rain. As they neared Kathy and Thad, the brindle's tail stopped wagging. He turned from Kathy and Thad to face D.J. and Alfred. The dog's hackles went up and he lowered his head.

D.J. stopped dead still. He threw out his right arm

to check his friend's advance. "Stop!"

Both boys stood still on the sidewalk.

The pit bull did not growl or bark; he just stood there with his hackles raised and his head lowered, watching the boys.

"Don't move!" D.J. whispered to Alfred.

"I'm too scared to move," Alfred whispered back, his voice shaky.

D.J. raised his voice slightly. "Kathy, back up slowly. Circle around him and get inside the store. You too, Thad."

Kathy hesitated, then answered, "This looks like one of the dogs that attacked Hero."

"Don't take any chances!" D.J. warned, his eyes never leaving the brindle. D.J.'s mind was racing, trying to think of something he could use as a weapon. He couldn't think of a thing except his belt, and that might only cause the dog to attack.

Out of the corner of his eye, D.J. saw Thad had automatically raised his hands in a defensive position. His coat sleeves stuck out of his tan raincoat.

Thad slowly backed up and around behind the pit bull toward the nearest store door. But Kathy didn't move.

"Nice doggie," she said soothingly. "Nice dog!"

D.J. was surprised to see the brindle's hackles lower. He turned his head to look up at Kathy. His tail wagged once.

"I think he likes me," she said.

"Well, he sure doesn't like us!" Alfred whispered.

D.J. raised his voice slightly. "Kathy, see if you can get him to go on after the other dogs. Quietly! Don't make any threatening moves."

She answered, "OK, but maybe he likes girls because boys and men have been mean to him." She bent slightly toward the dog. Her reddish-gold hair spilled over her shoulders, hiding her face.

"Don't try to figure him out!" D.J. warned. "Just see if he'll obey you and leave!"

"You're a nice dog," Kathy said gently. "But you'd better go on with your friends. Go on, now. Go!" She gently waved her left hand in the direction the two other dogs had gone.

The brindle's tail moved twice in short sweeps, then he turned and moved toward D.J. and Alfred. They held their breath as the dog eased past them. The boys' heads spun around so they could watch the pit bull. He broke into a quartering trot* and disappeared around a corner into an alley.

"Whew!" D.J. let out a great sigh of relief. "That was close! Kathy, are you all right?"

"Yes." She bent to examine her clothes. "I heard him snap, but he didn't touch me. There's not a mark on my jeans."

Thad ran out of the store waving his arms. "That dog's a menace! He could have bitten all of us!"

D.J. nodded. "What if it'd been a little kid who stepped on his foot? Or an old person, like my grandpa?"

Thad nodded vigorously. "Where's his owner? Why is he letting that dog run loose? I'm going to report this!"

D.J. said, "It won't do any good. Alfred and I were just over to the sheriff's office, but the animal control officer's not around."

"This is in the city, *not* the county. The police

should handle this! So I'm going to report it to them!"

D.J. was embarrassed. As a newspaper stringer, he should have remembered the difference between police and sheriff's duties. D.J. reacted by being more annoyed with Thad.

Thad didn't seem to notice. He smiled at Kathy. "Will I see you at the demonstration against the dam?"

"Just let me know for sure when it's scheduled. I've never been to an environmental demonstration before. See you later, Thad."

D.J. glared as Thad hurried off through the rain and wind. D.J. didn't like the way he was feeling, but it seemed nothing was going right. Well, at least nothing could go wrong with touring Yellow Dog.

The rain was coming down harder when Brother Paul dropped D.J. and Alfred off at the old ghost town. The lay pastor and Kathy planned to visit nearby friends but would return in half an hour to pick up the boys.

Yellow Dog was a remote, rural, foothill community on a side road, too tiny to even be listed on most maps. Yellow Dog was in the 1,500-foot elevation of the foothills, downstream from Indian Springs. The dam just below Yellow Dog would force the impounded water to back all the way up the canyon to the hermit's home in the 3,500-foot elevation close to Stoney Ridge.

D.J. and Alfred jumped under a long wooden overhang that ran the length of the main street's mostly closed stores. Most people had already moved away because the little town would soon be underwater when the dam was completed.

Alfred, always good at recalling facts, commented on what he remembered about the tiny community.

"Gold was first discovered here in 1850. But there wasn't much of it, so Yellow Dog didn't grow like many Gold Rush towns. Incidentally, it got its name from a miner who threw a rock at a stray yellow dog, and the rock turned out to have a nugget in it. Later, Yellow Dog was a Pony Express relay station and still later, a stagecoach stop."

Their boots clumped loudly on the wooden boardwalk under sagging overhangs built long ago against summer sun and winter rains. The friends passed the town's combination grocery store, cafe, and gas station.

D.J. pointed. "There're a couple of men sitting on that bench by the catalpa* tree. I'll interview them for the paper."

He unzipped his windbreaker and pulled a folded piece of paper from his shirt pocket. Mr. Kersten, the editor, had long ago warned the boy never to be without a way of making notes for a possible story.

"What'd I do with my pencil?" D.J. asked absently, feeling in his pants pocket.

Alfred didn't answer. "Most of the people who lived here have already moved away. There are more tourists here than residents."

D.J. continued to feel through his pockets while his eyes swept over the town. An old bell still hung in the open tower above the narrow firehouse. D.J. had toured the community before, so he remembered that the firehouse originally had been built for a hand-pulled hose cart. Later, there had been a horse-drawn engine, and finally the ancient Liberty fire truck that still served the community.

As D.J. pulled the windbreaker pockets out searching for his pencil, something sailed through the air. It landed on the broken asphalt pavement.

"What's that?" Alfred asked, squinting through his thick glasses at the object glistening in the rain.

"I picked it up at the hermit's," D.J. replied. He hurriedly stepped out from under the sidewalk shelter, picked up the object, and quickly jumped back under the shelter of the wooden sidewalk overhang.

"It's just a button, D.J."

"Yeah. Well, it's no good to me." He tossed it into an overflowing wooden trash barrel. "Oh, here's my pencil. Now I can take notes."

"Those men look sort of rough and mean," Alfred said uncertainly. "Long hair, beards, old clothes."

"People are people. Besides, whenever I tell people I work for a newspaper, they usually cooperate. You'll see."

He was right. The townspeople on the bench, after assuring themselves that D.J. really was a stringer for the county newspaper, began talking.

A prematurely bald man growled, "I wish somebody really would blow up that dam! It's driving me out of this town where I was born, and my father and his father before him!"

D.J. leaned forward from his seat on the edge of the bench. "Do all of you feel that way?"

Another man nodded, stroking his long, untidy brown and gray beard. "Sure do! We'd take it as a personal favor if someone did dynamite it."

The third person, a small, dark man with one missing front tooth, joined in. "Only one reason why somebody don't do it: because all the people downstream would drown!"

D.J. mused, "But the dam's not completed. There's no water behind it yet, so how could people drown?"

"I meant, 'later,' " the man answered. "All them demonstrators comin' up here act like it's already full of water."

D.J. thought of Kathy, who had always represented environmentalists to him. She was about as nice a person as D.J. knew. He asked, "What do you fellows think of environmentalists?"

The balding one said to the dirty-bearded man, "Tell him, Mike!"

Mike stroked his beard thoughtfully. "I used to work at a mill up north where a guy got badly hurt when his saw hit a spiked log as it came down the belt. The saw was spinning thousands of revolutions a minute.

"When the teeth hit that spike, the saw blade exploded. Pieces went through him like shrapnel* in 'Nam.* He was hurt really bad."

The balding man growled, "We've all worked the mills, so it could've happened to any of us!"

D.J. remembered reading about the incident. Radical activist environmentalists were blamed. Authorities said the radicals had gone through stands of timber waiting to be cut. They randomly drove railroad spikes so deeply into that log that only the head remained. Nobody in the mill saw the spike until it was too late.

"That was only one of several such incidents," Mike explained. "One police officer called them 'acts of terrorism.' "

The dark-complexioned man explained, "Don't get us wrong! We know there are good and bad people everywhere, including environmentalists. It's the radicals that scare us. Personally, though, I'd be glad if the dam did get blowed up."

Brother Paul drove up and honked. The boys thanked the townspeople and jumped into the pastor's car. By the time Brother Paul dropped D.J. off at home, it was just getting dark. The wind had died down about sunset, but the rain was still falling with a deadly, tireless purpose.

D.J. called the veterinary hospital. "No change? Still fighting the infection?"

Later in his room, he emptied the contents of his pockets on his bedside table. He automatically checked his clothes for Sunday School as he'd learned to do. He usually didn't have to wear a coat and tie, but he would on Easter. He took his only good white shirt from the dresser drawer and noticed that the top button was loose. He'd have to ask his stepmother to fix it. But he'd do that later. He turned to his desk.

After sorting through his scribbled notes, he began to work on a story about the people of Yellow Dog. He'd type up his article on the typewriter he'd won in a magazine contest.*

Two Mom knocked on D.J.'s door. "You're not forgetting your report for Sunday School, are you, D.J.?"

The boy groaned. He had forgotten. "I don't have

any ideas yet."

"You'd better think of something." Two Mom's footsteps faded back down the hallway.

The interruption had destroyed D.J.'s train of thought. He glanced at the notes, his fingers poised over the typewriter keys, thinking back to the interview in Yellow Dog.

Suddenly, D.J.'s head snapped up.

"Hey! That button I found at the hermit's. . . ."

He stood up. "But—that doesn't make sense!"

He raced into the living room where his father and stepmother were watching television.

"Dad! Two Mom! I know who framed the hermit with the dynamite and then bailed him out of jail! And why! He's going to be blamed when the dam blows up!"

Two Mom stood up in alarm, her short blond hair flying. "What're you saying?"

"Yeah!" Dad agreed, standing to face the excited boy. "What's the matter with you?"

"I've go to see Mr. Zeering right away and warn him!"

"Nobody's going any place in this rain! Now calm down and tell us what's got you so upset."

Chapter Nine

HERO WORSENS

D.J. hesitated, then plunged ahead. "I know who's trying to frame the hermit!"

Dad and Two Mom stared silently at D.J. and then exchanged glances. Dad cleared his throat and spoke gently but firmly.

"D.J., you're getting yourself all worked up over something you really don't know much about."

"Dad, I know—"

"You don't know anything!" Dad interrupted. He got up from his chair to face his son, who recoiled in surprise.

"D.J., you feel obliged to that old hermit because he saved your dog's life! But you really can't prove that the dynamite found at his place was planted there to make him look guilty! It could really be his powder!"

"Dad, if you'll just listen—"

"David Jonathan Dillon, you've got too wild an

imagination! I don't mind your trying to become a writer, but you've got to stop letting those wild ideas run away with your common sense!"

D.J. was so crushed and hurt he didn't know what to say. He looked into his father's stern blue eyes and knew it was useless. The boy glanced at his stepmother. She gently shook her head.

Dad spoke again. "I know that the hermit claimed he heard the Krockners at his shack just before he found his old dog killed. But that doesn't mean they planted the dynamite there!"

"Dad, I'm not trying to say—"

"That's enough, D.J.! Now, go back to your room and work on your report for Sunday!"

The boy ran back to his own room. He closed the door hard and threw himself across his bed.

He whispered fiercely as he buried his face in the pillow. "Why won't he listen to me? He doesn't even understand what I'm trying to say!"

Before he became a Christian, Dad Dillon would have slapped D.J. for what he'd just done. Dad sometimes still spoke sharply, especially if he was having troubles with work.

Right now, D.J. knew, was a slow time in selling firewood since the season was almost over, and Dad hadn't found a way to replace that income.

Still, the boy whispered, "Why couldn't he have just listened?"

After a while, D.J. changed into his pajamas and got into bed without praying. He didn't feel like talking to anybody, not even God.

D.J. closed his eyes, but he couldn't sleep. For hours, he lay on his bed staring unseeingly at the window. His thoughts were as dismal as the falling rain.

He momentarily thought about what he'd say Sunday when Mrs. Stagg called on him in class and he wasn't prepared. He hadn't been able to think of anything to write about. But that was nothing compared to all his other problems.

Would Hero live through the infection? What should D.J. do if the sheriff's office didn't do something about the Krockners and their three dogs, especially the brindle?

What should be done about the clue he'd found at the hermit's? Would it do any good to tell the sheriff's investigators?

"No! The only thing I can to is warn the hermit. But what will happen if the dam blows up before I can warn him? Will it be my fault?" he whispered into the soft darkness of his room. "Probably will be, so I've got to do something. But what?"

The sky occasionally exploded with lightning, but so far in the distance D.J. never heard the thunder. The only sound was the steady pounding of the downpour, hour after hour.

It was after 3 A.M. the last time D.J. looked at the red electronic letters on his dresser clock. He closed his eyes again. Finally, he slept fitfully.

He didn't awaken at dawn as he usually did. His stepsister's voice awakened D.J., and she was a late sleeper. He sat up in bed, startled to see it was after 8 o'clock. Two Mom had undoubtedly let him sleep in because it was Easter vacation. But D.J. had things to do—important things. He slid out of bed, ignoring the steady beating of rain against his window.

When D.J. finished dressing and came out of the bathroom, he heard Dad's car backing out of the garage. D.J. entered the kitchen in time to see Priscilla in the car with Dad.

Two Mom explained that Dad was driving Pris over to spend the day with one of her friends. Then Dad would go to the United States Forest Service to see about permits to cut wood for next winter.

D.J. nodded absently. "I've got to see the hermit right away."

"Now, D.J.—you're not going to start that again, are you?"

The boy blew noisily through his lips. "Then how about letting me go see Alfred?"

"In this rain?" Two Mom asked in surprise. She set a bowl on the kitchen table. "Whatever for?"

"I've got to talk to him," D.J. explained lamely. He didn't intend to get into another discussion like last night. He wished Alfred's parents had a phone.

"I don't know, D.J.," his stepmother said, raising a corner of the lace curtains over the kitchen window. "The radio said this morning that this storm has dumped so much water that there have been mud and rock slides on some roads. It's no time to be out."

D.J. remembered the hermit's prediction about a hard rain being able to start a monstrous landslide on the side of Lookout Peak. Still, the boy didn't want to think about that right now. He just wanted to see his best friend.

"I'll wear my weatherproof pants with the hooded jacket. I'll stay as dry as I would right here."

"You hate that rainsuit! You won't wear it to

school unless I force you." Two Mom turned to look at her stepson with serious eyes. "You really want to see Alfred that much?"

"Yes, I do," he said quietly. "So can I go?"

"May I?" Two Mom corrected him automatically. "Well, if it's that important—"

"Thanks, Two Mom!" He turned to rush out of the room, but his stepmother stopped him.

"But you've got to eat breakfast first!"

"I'll eat right after I call the vet."

He got right through to Dr. Barner. She said, "Oh, hello, D.J. I was just going to phone you."

Her tone made D.J.'s heart almost stop. "Is Hero OK?" the boy asked.

"That's why I was going to call."

There was no doubt; her voice suggested bad news. Dr. Barner paused, then continued with a gentler tone. But her words cut through the boy like a knife.

"I'm sorry, D.J., but the infection is not responding to the stronger antibiotics."

D.J. sucked in his breath as though he'd been hit in the stomach. "You mean he's worse?"

"Unfortunately, yes. D.J., I have to ask—do you want Hero put to sleep? It would be totally painless—"

"NO!" D.J.'s explosive word interrupted her. "NO! You keep trying! He'll make it!"

He couldn't speak anymore because his whole body seemed about to burst. D.J. fought back tears that leaped to his eyes. He hung up the receiver and leaned his forehead against the wall.

He closed his eyes against the terrible hurt and

sadness. In that pain, D.J. forgot about the hermit and what he wanted to warn him about.

"I can't even go be with Hero!" he groaned.

He felt Two Mom's hand gently touch his left forearm. "I'm sorry," she whispered. "I can't reach your father, and the Milfords don't have a phone. But I'll phone Brother Paul and see if he can drive you to Indian Springs to see your dog."

Wordlessly, D.J. nodded as his stepmother lifted the receiver and dialed. A moment later she gently replaced the instrument.

"There's no answer. The Staggs must have all gone someplace."

D.J. spun away from the wall, his eyes hot with tears of frustration and anger. "It's the Krockners' fault! And their dogs'!"

"Now, D.J.! Enough! You'll feel better after you've talked with Alfred. Go get dressed while I make breakfast."

Reluctantly, the boy went to his room and dressed warmly in a heavy coat, pants, and boots with waterproof soles. When he reentered the kitchen, he was clothed totally in waterproof blue rain pants and matching jacket with the hood hanging down in back. The outfit made loud rustling noises as he walked.

The boy was anxious to be off, but he knew better than to try leaving without breakfast. Reluctantly, he sank into a chair.

Two Mom placed a steaming bowl before him. "Say the blessing and eat."

He started to say, "I don't feel like it," but knew that wouldn't please his stepmother. He bowed his head quickly, but he was too angry to pray. He raised his head, ate fast, and soon stood up, thinking of Hero and what the Krockners had done to him.

As he zipped up his rain jacket, Two Mom asked, "Are you all right?"

"I'm OK." His voice was flat, cold, and numb as he was all over.

"I know how you hurt over your little dog, but your face looks angry."

"I *am* angry! I'm plain mad! Those people and their dogs did this to Hero and nobody's doing a thing about it!"

He started for the front door. He pulled the hood over his head. A stiff bill stuck out in front, making it hard to see well.

"D.J., don't do anything that your father or I wouldn't approve of! You promised your father! And remember what the Bible says about vengeance."

The boy didn't reply. He stepped out into the hard rain and started running.

"I don't care! I've got to do what I've got to do," he whispered fiercely. Then he remembered and added, "But first I've got to warn the hermit—and fast!"

Chapter Ten

A TERRIBLE SIGHT IN THE MEADOW

Alfred's mother was also reluctant to let her son go out in the heavy rain. D.J. explained what the vet had said about Hero's infection being worse. Mrs. Milford understood the boys needed time alone to talk.

Alfred dressed in a green rainsuit that he hated as much as D.J. did his blue one. The boys clomped down the high steps from the Milfords' rented house. D.J. wanted to see the hermit, but first he had to get Alfred alone to explain things to him.

"What're Hero's chances?" Alfred asked, peering over the top of his thick glasses. They had fogged up from coming out of the warm house into the crisp mountain air.

D.J. shrugged. "I don't know. I feel so helpless!" He headed through the rain toward the sheltered northern side of the little grocery store near the road.

"Hero'll be OK, D.J."

"I hope so! Maybe if he could see me he'd feel

better. But I can't even get over to the vet's hospital. And in the meantime, the Krockners and their dogs are still running free!"

"D.J., there's nothing you—"

"I know!" D.J. interrupted. He snapped his fingers. "Oh, something else I've got to tell you!"

"What?"

"Remember that button I pulled out of my pocket yesterday at Yellow Dog?"

"Yeah."

"I'd found it at the hermit's."

"So?"

"It's a clue!"

His friend stopped short in the rain. "A clue to what?"

"To the ones who planted the dynamite at the hermit's place and got him jailed for threatening to blow up the dam!"

"What do you mean?"

"Somebody dropped it when they went to Mr. Zeering's place to plant the dynamite that got him arrested."

"Who? The Krockners?"

D.J. was almost trembling with the excitement of what he knew. "No, not *them!* Thad Thorkell and his father!"

"The environmentalists? D.J., are you nuts?"

"No, it makes perfect sense!"

"Not to me!"

"Sure it does! Listen—who would've had the money to get Mr. Zeering bailed out of jail?"

Alfred pushed his glasses up on his nose with an automatic thrust of his right thumb. "Not the

Krockners. They don't even have enough money to feed their dogs well!"

"Exactly! But the Thorkells *do!* And I think they're radical environmentalists like those who've spiked trees and done other terrible things to hurt people."

Alfred shrugged doubtfully. "I don't know, D.J. Why would the Thorkells want to frame the hermit and then turn around and bail him out of jail?"

"That's exactly why they did it! Don't you see? What if they were setting things up so that when the dam was blown, Mr. Zeering would be arrested for it? He's already been jailed once. Wouldn't everyone be convinced he really was guilty?

"And didn't he say he'd never go back to jail? So that means he probably would end up dead, falsely blamed, and never be able to clear his name. Doesn't that make sense?"

Alfred frowned. "Well, maybe. But what's that got to do with the button you found?"

"It's got to be Thad's. The first time we saw him at the vet's I noticed his coat. Then in Indian Springs when the brindle snapped at Kathy, I saw that he was missing a button. Thad must have lost it when he was planting the dynamite at the hermit's!"

Alfred shook his head, throwing rainwater from his waterproof hood. "I don't know, D.J. Thad could have lost the button, but somebody might have found it and dropped it at the hermit's. Like the Krockners."

"Maybe you're right. But what's important right now is that we warn Mr. Zeering."

"In this weather?"

"We don't know when the Thorkells might try to blow up the dam. They could've already planted the dynamite. They could blow it up today!

"And the hermit said he was never going back to jail—that he'd die first! Come on, Alfred. We've got no time to waste!"

The dreary rain almost made the hermit's cabin invisible against the dense ponderosas, sugar pines, and black oaks. As D.J. and Alfred approached the front porch, a voice cracked behind them.

"Don't move! Don't move nary a hair! This here shotgun's loaded with double-ought buckshot!"*

D.J.'s heart instantly leaped into a wild gallop. He raised his hands and saw Alfred doing the same.

"Mr. Zeering?" D.J. asked, hearing his voice echo inside the waterproof hood of his blue rainsuit. "Mr. Zeering, it's us—D.J. Dillon and Alfred Milford!"

"Turn around slow-like so's I kin see yore faces under all them rainsuits!"

Carefully, the boys turned. D.J. blinked. The old hermit didn't have a gun. He held a pick handle in his wet hands. Rain trickled from his old hat and ran down his weathered face. He wore an ancient black rain slicker that covered him from shoulders to knees.

"Well, now!" Mr. Zeering managed a smile. "I recken it is you two boys! For a minute there, I thought I'd ketched me two more polecats! Put your hands down, and let's all git up on the porch."

The boys obeyed, though the porch roof leaked so bad it wasn't much drier there than out in the weather.

D.J. asked, "What'd you mean about catching two more polecats, Mr. Zeering?"

"Wait'll I open the door and ye'll see." The old hermit was almost gleeful, D.J. noticed. The splintery door swung open on rusted hinges. "You varmints kin come out now."

By the light of a kerosene lamp inside on the homemade table, D.J. saw two shadows move. A moment later, Thad Thorkell and his father scooted to the doorway. Their hands and feet were bound with old, dirty rope.

"Hey!" D.J. exclaimed. "Alfred and I were just coming to warn you about them! But—how'd you catch them?"

The old hermit chuckled and lightly tapped the heavy end of the hardwood pick handle in his open left palm. "I heerd someone a'sneakin' around. Figured it was them other fellers and their dogs again. Instead, I found these two! They was a'tryin' to hide some blasting caps* in the rafters of my shed over there!

"Hee! Hee!" Mr. Zeering's glee was expressed in light laughter. "Outsmarted them, I did! I'd already been a'studyin' on who might've paid my bail, and the answer come up this polecat—and his young'un. But I couldn't figure out why until I caught 'em. Was a'goin' to blow up the dam, they was, and blame me!"

D.J. nodded in agreement and started to mention the button, but Mr. Thorkell spoke first. "We're innocent!"

"Right!" Thad said. "We keep trying to tell this wild-eyed old hermit—"

Mr. Thorkell interrupted his son's sentence. "A confession obtained under duress* won't hold up in court! We're not guilty, as we've been trying to tell you! But you won't listen!"

"I don't rightly know the meaning of that there *duress* word," the hermit said with a smile. "But you're a'goin' to jail! See how you like it!"

D.J. saw Mr. Thorkell sigh. "OK, then let's get started! We'll get a lawyer and prove we're innocent!"

The hermit shook his head. "No, siree bob! I'm not a'gonna take a chance y'all would try to get away from me. D.J., would you and Alfred go get the law and bring them here?"

Soon the boys were hurrying back toward town. The shortest way lay across the meadows directly underneath the southeast side of Lookout Peak. D.J. was so excited he didn't think about the hermit's warning of a possible slide.

The boys started across the first open meadow. It sloped steeply toward the rain-soaked side of Lookout Peak. A stand of ponderosa trees marked the end of the meadow before the mountain rose sharply upward.

As the boys approached a rain-carved gully near the middle of the meadow, Alfred stopped abruptly. He pointed beyond the line of pines. "Is it my imagination, or is there a break up high on the side of that mountain?"

D.J. followed his friend's finger. D.J. froze in fright at the sight. There definitely was a crack about a foot across high up on the shoulder of that massive mountain. There had been no break the last time D.J. had seen the mountain.

The boys quickly considered the situation, remembering the hermit's warning.

As D.J. and Alfred continued across the meadow,
every step took them closer to the crack. They'd be
under the danger until they'd climbed beyond it toward the parking lot by the cross on top of the peak.

If the boys backtracked to where it was safe, it'd
be at least another hour before they reached a
paved road. That might be enough time for the
Thorkells to try escaping from the hermit.

"What do you think, D.J.?" Alfred asked, still
squinting up at the mountain. "Should we—listen!"

D.J. lowered his eyes from the mountain to the
stand of timber beyond the meadow. The brindle
pit bull and the two larger dogs were trotting out of
the trees, followed by Beau and Rulon Krockner.
They had left the second meadow divided from the
first where the boys were by a stand of trees.

As they entered the meadow where D.J. and Alfred stood, D.J. noticed that the father carried what
looked like three road flares taped together. D.J.
had seen individual flares scattered along rural
mountain roads where the highway patrol had
marked an accident.

At the same instant, D.J. heard a faint rumble like
distant thunder. He glanced up in time to see a
crack slowly open in the massive mountainside. A
piece of earth about the size of a football field
broke loose.

Alfred whispered in awe, "What is it?"

"Looks like—mud," D.J. threw back his rain
hood so he could get a better look. "It is mud! The
hermit was right!"

The huge chunk of wet earth looked almost like monstrous, gooey, chocolate cake batter pouring from a giant pan. But the slide gained momentum as it neared the foot of the mountain.

D.J. stood uncertainly for a moment, fascinated at the strange sight. Then he dropped his eyes to the Krockners and their dogs.

They were moving into the open meadow, unaware of the danger slipping up behind them. D.J. realized their vision of the slide was blocked by the trees immediately behind them.

The brindle caught sight of D.J. and Alfred and began running silently, purposefully toward them. There were no trees in the open meadow, no places for the boys to run or hide. The two other dogs started barking furiously and raced after the brindle.

"D.J., let's get out of here!" Alfred's voice cracked with fear.

For a moment, D.J. hesitated. His eyes darted up to the mountainside. The massive mud slide was gaining speed, scooping out small trees and dislodging boulders. The front of the slide hit the edge of the forest. This was behind the Krockners and against the base of the great mountain. D.J. and Alfred could see clearly what was happening, but the Krockners could not.

D.J. saw the tops of young ponderosas quiver as the shock of the mud slide hit their trunks. Then the trees were uprooted and fell slowly into the rest of the forest.

The two Krockners didn't call off their dogs. Father and son just kept walking, totally unaware of the mud slide bearing silently down behind them.

D.J. cupped his hands over his mouth and yelled.
"Hey! Look out!" He pointed frantically toward the
oozing mound of mud.

The Krockners didn't seem to notice.

"They can't hear you!" Alfred cried. "And they're
not calling off their dogs!"

The dogs were closing fast now, nearing the
helpless D.J. and Alfred.

Suddenly, the Krockners turned to look behind
them. A split second later, D.J. heard the sound of
the falling trees and knew that was what had made
father and son turn.

D.J. saw the father drop his bundle of road
flares. Both Krockners started running downhill toward the canyon rim.

"No!" D.J. yelled. "Not that way! You can't outrun
it that way! Run sideways up the hill!"

A finger of mud, like a giant tentacle from an oc-
topus, suddenly snaked around the front of the forest. With nothing to slow its race across the steeply
slanted open meadow, the ugly brown mass slith-
ered faster and faster toward the running dogs.

They were furiously closing in on D.J. and Alfred
and didn't see the danger. The mud caught the
dogs from behind. D.J. heard startled yelps and saw
all three dogs paddling frantically, trying to keep
their heads up. Then the two big dogs went under.

A second later, the main body of mud shot out
from the edge of the forest. Trees, logs, brush, and
boulders ground along in the powerful mass shooting across the meadow.

The two sections of mud were like great pincers
resembling a giant hand. The forefinger had been

thrust out first, catching the dogs. Then the second, larger section closed in like a thumb and palm. When they touched, it was like a hand closing. The brindle was caught when the thumb and finger made contact. The pit bull was sucked out of sight.

D.J.'s eyes shot back to the Krockners. A wall of mud ten feet high was rushing upon them from behind.

"Don't run downhill!" D.J. screamed again.

"They can't hear you, D.J.!"

As the boys watched helplessly, the massive mud slide caught the running Krockners. They were lifted as if on a giant ocean wave. The man and boy vanished behind a newly uprooted ponderosa tumbling in the slide.

"Oh, no!" D.J. whispered.

Moments later, the mud reached the edge of the canyon at the meadow's end and poured thickly over the sides. In seconds, it was gone, leaving only an inch-deep, ugly, brown stain on the meadow and a shattered stand of twisted or flattened trees.

D.J. stared at the scene in disbelief. The hated Krockners and their dogs had vanished without a trace!

Chapter Eleven

BURIED ALIVE!

D.J. stood in stunned silence for a moment.

For days, he had desperately wanted the Krockners and their dogs to suffer as Hero had. Now, in seconds, in a way the boy would never have guessed possible, the dogs and people who had attacked Hero were gone, swept away in a gigantic natural disaster.

The terrible impact of what had happened made D.J. reel. He staggered backward and turned away.

"I'm going to be sick," he told Alfred.

"You wanted revenge on all of them for what they did to Hero. You got revenge."

"But not that way!" D.J. cried. "I wouldn't have wished that—listen!"

D.J. lifted his neck high above the blue rain hood he'd thrown off earlier. He cocked his head to listen. The rain fell unheeded on the boy's face.

"What?" Alfred whispered.

"I thought . . . yes! Hear it? Somebody's calling!"

"The Krockners?"

"Yes! They're alive! Or one of them!"

He started to run into the brown stain, but the inch-deep mud sucked at his boots. He fell forward into the gunk. He forced himself up, tearing off the muddy rain gear. Alfred did the same. They dropped the rain slickers in the mud and sloshed across the meadow.

D.J. glanced up through the falling rain at the place where the slide had started. He stopped in his tracks.

"Alfred, look!" D.J.'s mouth was so dry from fear that his tongue felt like a dry bone clacking in a box. "See? The rest of the mountain might slide down on us!"

The great mountain's southeastern slope showed an ugly scar where the mud slide had broken away. But a section at least ten times larger still clung precariously to the mountain's shoulder. The potential slide glistened wetly and menacingly. Rivulets of water poured down the shiny face. Rain fell harder.

"You're right!" Alfred agreed. "We'd better get out of here!" He turned back toward the hermit's place.

D.J. hesitated, his mind spinning. A faint cry came from beyond a downed ponderosa tree across the meadow.

"Help!"

The mountain boy's thoughts whirled faster. *Those Krockners aren't worth risking my life for! They deserve what they got!*

"HELP!"

To save his own life, D.J. only had to turn away, and the revenge he had wanted would be complete. But suddenly, the boy turned to Alfred.

"I just can't leave them—no matter what they did!" D.J. sloshed across the muddy meadow.

"Then I'm going with you!" Alfred cried.

At the edge of what was left of the timber, the friends found two human figures, totally covered with mud. One had been tossed like a wet bag of sawdust into the branches of a small black oak. The tree had been uprooted and lay on the muddy ground. The other person sagged weakly across a piece of lightning-blasted snag.*

Only the muddy, matted beard made it possible to recognize that this was Beau Krockner. His arms flopped loosely with the weight of great globs of heavy, gooey mud. What was left of his coat clung wetly to his upper body. Muddy pants drooped around his knees. His wide eyes stared out of a muddy face.

A few feet away, his son coughed hoarsely in the black oak's branches. Except for a piece of his jacket still around his right shoulder, Rulon's outer clothes and one high-topped shoe had been torn off. Only the scrap of his jacket, muddy underclothes, one sock, and one shoe remained.

"I—can't breathe!" Rulon gasped between coughing spasms.

"I'm coming!" D.J. yelled. He waded rapidly through ankle-deep mud toward Rulon. D.J. called over his shoulder, "Alfred, see if you can help Beau toward high ground in case the rest of that mud slides down!"

Moments later, D.J. had swept mud from the long-haired boy's face and mouth. Rulon took great, gasping breaths.

He managed to gasp, "I thought I was a goner!"

D.J. asked, "You OK?" He tried to help Rulon to his feet.

"I think so." The voice came hoarsely from a muddy face. "How about my old man?"

"He's OK. Alfred's helping him. Come on—we've got to get out of here!"

"I got to . . . rest . . . a little first."

"There's no time! Here, let me help you up."

Alfred was beside D.J., holding Beau's muddy right arm over his shoulder. "Ready, D.J.?"

"Yes. Come on, both of you! Let's get out of here!" D.J. glanced fearfully up at Lookout Peak, then pointed straight ahead, to the left of the mountain. "We'll be safe in those rocks."

His eyes focused on the designated area. It seemed like a long way off, past the remnants of the timber stand and across another meadow.

"Leave us be!" Beau growled. "The danger's past."

"Yeah!" Rulon said, rubbing mud from his mouth with the back of a gritty hand. "Quit bothering us! We're going to rest! Where're my dogs?"

D.J. felt a surge of annoyance. The Krockners were about as ornery now as ever. Still, D.J. tried to explain quietly though he wanted to shout at the muddy pair.

"I saw the dogs go under when the mud slide caught them."

"All three?" Rulon asked in surprise.

D.J. nodded but tried to point out the remaining danger on the mountainside. The father and son didn't listen. They began cursing.

Between his more violent words, Beau yelled, "Them was the best dogs a man ever had, especially Boog! If you two wasn't out there a'tormentin' him and the others—"

D.J. interrupted, his voice shaking with anger. "Look—I'm trying to tell you something! See where the slide started up on the mountainside?"

The Krockners glanced upward. The great mountain's southeastern slope showed an ugly scar where the mud slide had originated.

Beau Krockner shrugged. "So what?"

D.J. had to swallow hard to keep his voice even. "That's where the mud slide came from. But look over to the left. If that big section up there breaks off while we're down here. . . ." He let his sentence remain unfinished.

Beau again glanced up at the mountainside. Ninety percent of that slide was still up there, glistening wetly and menacingly.

"Yeah, I see what you mean." Beau said, shoving himself to his feet. "Come on, Rulon. Let's get out of here!"

The father and son started a weak, staggering run toward the high ground. D.J. shook his head in disbelief. "No concern for us at all, Alfred," D.J. muttered.

He trotted alongside Alfred, their boots nearly sucked off with every step. "Makes you wonder why we bothered, doesn't it, D.J.?"

"I never saw more ungrateful people," D.J. admitted. "But we'd better save our breath for climbing."

In a few minutes, the four were clear of the mud slide's path and in another smaller open meadow just below a brushy area of tumbled rocks. Beau and Rulon were already scrambling hand over hand up the steep incline toward the safety of the rock outcropping.

D.J. glanced fearfully up at the side of the mountain. "Another few minutes," he said with forced cheerfulness. "And we'll be up high enough that even if the rest of the mountain lets go, we'll be safe."

"Yuck!" Alfred exclaimed. "Look where we've got to climb! It's covered with mountain misery! Our clothes and hands will stink for a year!"

"Use it to pull yourself up and never mind about the smell! It'll—"

D.J. broke off sharply as the earth seemed to tremble beneath his feet. *Earthquake? No, not in this part of California.* Automatically, the boy's eyes flickered upward to the mountainside.

Something didn't look right.

He blinked through the falling rain, unable to think what was different.

Then he realized what it was. The whole side of the mountain was gone!"

Fearfully, D.J. glanced down. An enormous wall of mud, perhaps thirty feet high and a quarter mile across, was hurtling away from the base of the mountain. The ugly, brown mass was sliding into a box canyon that opened like a funnel's mouth into the open meadow. The forced confinement sent the mud shooting down like logs in a water flume.

"Look!" The word exploded from D.J.'s mouth. He held on to some of the evil-smelling mountain misery with one hand and pointed with the other.

From their higher position in the rocky brush, the Krockners stopped their desperate climb.

Rulon's voice was almost a squeak from fright. "Higher than a housetop! And comin' like a runaway locomotive!"

"Shut up and climb, you idjit!" the father snapped.

"Climb, Alfred!" D.J. cried, scrambling to pull himself up toward the safety of the rock outcropping. He ignored the cuts on his fingers and the pains in his body and legs where brush punched through his clothing.

Out of the corner of his eyes, D.J. could see Alfred frantically pulling himself up. D.J. shot a quick glance toward the mud slide.

It was huge, much more awesome than the first one. This massive mud flow shot out from the small box canyon and sluiced across the meadow like a monstrous flood of dirty water. It seemed more like a flash flood than a mountain of mud, except this made a strange, unearthly sound and moved more slowly.

D.J. heard grinding noises mixed with the cracking of hundred-foot-tall trees as they were violently uprooted and crashed into the swirling brown mass of boulders, brush, and dead snags.

"Hurry, D.J.!" Alfred's voice was ragged with uneven breathing.

"I am! I AM!" D.J. heard almost sobbing sounds and realized he was making that noise as he scrambled hand over hand up the rocky hill. His nostrils were filled with the stench of mountain misery. D.J.'s muddy boots slipped on the rocks, and he slid backward on his stomach toward the meadow.

"Hang on, D.J.!" Alfred cried.

D.J. grasped desperately for rocks and crevices, but his grip was torn loose. He jabbed his foot into a big bush and came to a jarring halt.

"Thanks, Lord!" D.J. began climbing faster, regaining the ground he'd lost in the slide. His breath came in gulps of desperation.

D.J.'s slip had put Alfred a dozen feet ahead of him and off to the right. Alfred's glasses were knocked off one ear. Without those thick lenses, Alfred couldn't see ten feet. He automatically shoved the glasses back into place with a very muddy right thumb.

"You OK, D.J.?"

"Yes! Keep climbing!"

Beau Krockner's voice called. "Almost there!"

D.J. glanced up. The father and son were well up the mountain's slick side. Alfred was just behind them. D.J. was desperately trying to catch up.

The ground trembled beneath him as the wall of mud slid across the little meadow, burying it under a garage-high mass. In seconds, D.J. heard the leading edge slide by below. It made a strange hissing noise, something like an angry snake.

Alfred cried, "We're going to make it!"

D.J. glanced up in happy joy. The Krockners had

reached the safety of the high rock outcropping. The father had already turned around and was leaning against a great boulder to catch his breath.

Rulon jumped to his feet and let out a joyful yell. "I made it, Pop!"

Through the rain, D.J. caught a fragmentary glimpse of the Easter cross standing on top of Lookout Peak off to the right.

"O-h-h-h . . . !"

The startled shriek jerked D.J.'s eyes toward the Krockners. Rulon's feet had shot out from under him. He landed hard on his backside. Instantly, in a sitting position, he started sliding out of control! He shot down the slick mountainside as fast as a toboggan in snow!

"Help me-e-e-e-e!" Rulon screamed as his speed increased.

But it was too late for his father to help. In a second, the boy's body hurtled past Alfred, shooting down toward D.J. like a greased otter on a water slide.

D.J. reacted instinctively. He held on to a clump of mountain misery with his left hand. He grabbed wildly at Rulon as he zipped by. D.J.'s muddy hand closed on what was left of Rulon's torn, muddy jacket.

Rulon's momentum jerked D.J.'s left hand free of his hold on the plant. In an instant, D.J. was also sliding headfirst down the mountain, clinging to Rulon's tattered coat.

"Grab something!" D.J. yelled as Rulon's sliding body threw mud into D.J.'s face.

"I'm . . . trying!"

With his free hand, D.J. also tried to grab some-thing, but the two splashed faster and faster down the slippery mountainside.

D.J.'s trailing left boot toe snagged momentarily into some brush. Instantly, D.J. jammed his foot down hard, hoping to hook into the heart of the bush and stop their slide.

It worked!

D.J. was almost torn apart from the force of Rulon's body zipping ahead and the sudden yanking on his own leg from behind. He groaned, closed his eyes against the pain, and held on. The bush came partway out of the soaked ground, then the roots held.

The wild ride stopped. D.J. opened his eyes. He was still holding tightly to the tattered remnants of Rulon's muddy coat.

Rulon hauled himself behind a small boulder only inches from the river of mud slithering by.

D.J. cautiously let go of Rulon's coat. D.J. used both hands to grip the biggest clump of mountain misery he could reach. Slowly, he lifted his leg free of the brush that had stopped their headlong plunge down the mountain.

Alfred called from above and behind. "Everybody OK?"

D.J. saw Rulon wave weakly in acknowledgment.

Beau shouted, "Hold still, Rulon! I'm a'comin'!"

"Me, too!" Alfred cried. "Hang on, D.J.!"

"No!" D.J. was surprised how weak his voice sounded. He tried to pull himself to a sitting posi-tion, using the smelly clump of mountain misery. "The mud will soon pass and we'll be OK!"

A sick sensation shot through D.J. as the rain-soaked roots of the plant he held suddenly let go with dull snapping sounds and came loose in his hands!

"O Lord—no!"

D.J. grabbed wildly for something else to hang on to, but it was too late. Before Rulon could react, D.J. flashed past him. D.J. shot headfirst onto the crest of the passing wall of mud!

He automatically took a deep breath and closed his eyes. The cold, thick mass slid over his face. He was instantly sucked down into a crushing, suffocating blackness.

D.J. was buried alive in a mountain of mud!

Chapter Twelve

THE OTHER SIDE OF NOTHING

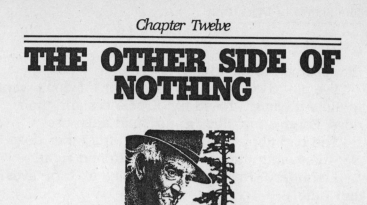

D.J. fought against instant panic. He instinctively reached out both arms in a swimming motion, trying to get control. He managed to pull his left arm back where it was imprisoned against his body. The right arm was thrust out and upward, but D.J. couldn't pull it back against the crushing cocoon of mud. He couldn't tell where his right hand was. It had no feeling.

He held his breath and kicked in a desperate drive upward toward air and light. Instead, D.J. felt himself held down. He tumbled around slowly like a wet towel in his stepmother's glass-door washing machine.

He felt his body weakening. *I'm dying!* The thought hit with the force of a baseball bat across the nose. Immediately, he shook off the idea.

D.J. had heard that the lives of dying people flashed before their eyes. D.J.'s own thoughts flickered like a strobe light, one after the other, so fast they seemed to blend into one.

"I've got to get some air—fast! Lord, I don't want to die! All week, I hated the Krockners and their dogs. Forgive me! But I'm not mad anymore!

"Too bad about the brindle and the other dogs. Not their fault; they just weren't trained right.

"I wonder if Hero's going to make it? If he lives and I die. . . .

"The hermit! Those Thorkells might get away from him, and—hey! What was Beau Krockner carrying when the first mud slide . . . ?"

D.J. tried to hold onto the thought, but it drifted away, fragile as a dragonfly's wing.

He was starting to lose consciousness. The pressure of the mud felt less crushing. It didn't bother D.J. as much. "I'm getting so tired," he thought dreamily. He felt himself drifting, drifting into nothingness.

It seemed he was looking down on the boy known as D.J. Dillon, suffocating in a river of mud.

Something jarred him so hard his drifting thoughts were torn away. He felt himself being yanked by his right hand, the one he hadn't been able to feel.

As though from a long way off, he felt something moving very fast down from the hand to the arm to the top of his head; on to his forehead, his eyes, nose, and mouth. Something wet like rain hit his face.

Suddenly, he couldn't control his breath any-more. His tortured lungs seemed to explode. He blew out mightily, spewing mud. Instantly, he sucked in a great, ragged gulp of air. It was filled with mud that sent him into a fearful coughing spasm.

Dimly, still as though from a great distance, D.J. heard Beau Krockner's voice. "He's alive!"

"Thank God!" That was Alfred.

D.J. tried to open his eyes, but the coughing and gasping took over. Between coughs, D.J. sucked in gulps of air. Each breath came easier. He felt cold air on his cheeks.

His head cleared with the delight in each breath. He tried to say, "Thanks, Lord," but it came out as a sobbing sound of pure joy at being able to breathe.

The coughing eased. D.J. forced his eyes open. He felt tears running down his gritty cheeks. Overhead, the sky was clearing. The sun broke through the retreating clouds. A sunbeam reflected off something high up on a mountaintop. He recognized the cross.

His eyes turned toward a movement closer to him. "Alfred, is that you?" The words were weak and quavering.

Alfred's grin answered him. Then D.J. recognized Beau Krockner and Rulon. Their faces seemed suspended between earth and sky as they stared down at him.

"You done saved my boy's life," Beau said softly. "I'm beholdin' to you for that."

It took a moment for D.J. to remember what had happened. Then he pushed himself up to a sitting position. He was surprised to see the mud's power had stripped him of his coat, shirt, and undershirt.

D.J. felt a strange weight at his waist. He glanced down and saw his belt had trapped pounds of mud around his middle. Absently, the boy began brushing the mud away, his eyes moving on to his feet.

He could see his boot prints where he'd been dragged up from the residue of mud to a small rocky ledge in the middle of a smelly patch of mountain misery.

An ugly brown trail a few inches thick showed on the meadow to where the mud wall had poured over the canyon rim toward the river.

D.J. looked at the Krockners and Alfred. They were almost as muddy as D.J.

"Thanks," D.J. said. Then he frowned, remembering.

"How'd you find me?"

"Beau saw your right hand sticking up." Alfred said, squatting to look into his friend's face.

D.J. turned his eyes upon the long-haired man. "You pulled me out?"

"I owed you for saving Rulon. Besides, they helped." Beau nodded at his son and Alfred.

Rulon added, "The mud carried you back against the mountainside here. When the slide started going over the canyon, the mud got shallow real fast. That's when Pop saw your hand."

D.J. swallowed hard. "I'm eternally thankful."

"Let's get you home," Beau Krockner said.

D.J. straightened up. "Yeah! I've got to check on Hero! Maybe he's OK by now!"

D.J. turned to look at Alfred and the Krockners and suddenly remembered something.

"Hey! I almost forgot! The hermit's holding the Thorkells for the sheriff! They framed him into going to jail for threatening to blow up the dam! We've got to get to a phone!"

D.J. got weakly to his feet, surprised at how sore

he felt all over. He glanced down and saw dozens
of cuts and bruises mixed with the mud starting to
harden over his body.

Spurred on by the need to call the sheriff for Mr.
Zeering, D.J. forced himself to start moving. Then,
abruptly, he stopped and stared across the two
muddy meadows.

Alfred asked, "What's the matter?"

"I was thinking," D.J. replied, seeing something
in his mind's eye; a picture of something that had
happened just before the first mud slide hit.

"What?" Alfred insisted.

D.J. frowned and shook his head. "I—don't know.
Something—oh! Yes, of course! They didn't do it."

"Who didn't do what?" Alfred asked.

"The Thorkells! They didn't plant that dynamite
so the hermit would get blamed!"

"They didn't?" Alfred asked in surprise. "Then
who did?"

D.J. didn't answer. His thoughts leaped furiously
for something he couldn't quite pin down.

D.J. saw the Krockners exchange glances, but he
didn't pay much attention. His memory flashed
back to when he'd first seen the Krockners ap-
proaching the big meadow with the three dogs.
They had charged toward D.J. and Alfred. Beau had
been carrying something, something he dropped
when the first small mud slide raced up behind
them. Roadside flares! That's what D.J. had thought.
Now he knew better.

Beau said softly, "You done figgered it out finally,
ain't you?"

"Figured what out?" Alfred demanded.

"Nothing!" D.J. said, his mouth suddenly dry from fear.

"I see it in your eyes," Beau said. "Well, go ahead and spit it out 'cause you done saved my boy's hide, and I'm not a'goin' to hurt you none, nor yore friend."

D.J. hesitated, his mind still whirling. He glanced at Rulon.

He was a muddy mess with globs of the sticky brown stuff clinging to his long hair. "You heard my pop!" Rulon said. "Tell us!"

D.J. nervously cleared his throat. "Weren't those sticks of dynamite you were carrying when the first slide caught you?"

Rulon stirred uneasily, but his father laid a restraining hand on the boy's arm.

"Sure was! You know what we was a'goin' to do with 'em too, don't you?"

D.J. slowly nodded. "I think so. What fooled me was that I had thought Thad Thorkell and his father were the ones."

Alfred demanded, "What're you talking about, D.J.?"

He didn't answer because something else didn't make sense. His mind seemed to have grasped a truth only to have it ripped to shreds a moment later.

Besides, wasn't he taking too great a risk to voice the wild thoughts zipping through his mind?

"Well, go on!" Beau insisted.

D.J. tried to slow his ideas, to sort them out. He was still foggy-brained from being buried alive in the mud. But as his mind slowly cleared, he spoke.

"You were the ones who tried to get the hermit blamed for the bomb threats."

Alfred exclaimed, "D.J.! What're you saying?"

Rulon demanded, "What makes you say that?"

D.J. frowned, still trying to piece things together right. But they didn't quite fit. "It's only a guess," D.J. admitted. "I think you found Thad's coat button and deliberately left it at the hermit's when you planted the dynamite the sheriff's deputies found."

"Ha! A lot you know!" Rulon said.

"Shut up!" the father snapped. "Let D.J. go on."

D.J. hesitated, feeling terrible about what he was thinking, knowing that the Krockners had just saved his life. It was an awful predicament for D.J. Still, he had to explain.

"You were setting the hermit up to take the blame when the dam would finally be blown up. On the other hand, you two don't strike me. . . ." D.J. stopped uncertainly.

The mixed-up thoughts flashed and twisted in D.J.'s mind. Something still didn't make sense. But what was it?

Beau asked through his muddy, caked beard, "What about bailing the old hermit out of jail?"

D.J. frowned. "I didn't think you had the money to bail him out, but somehow, you must have. Otherwise, Mr. Zeering wouldn't have been free when the dam really blew."

The Krockners exchanged glances. The father nodded. "That's what you think, is it?"

D.J. went on, his mind tumbling with things that he couldn't quite grasp. "Then this morning, the Thorkells must have gone to tell the old man that they hadn't bailed him out; maybe to ask him to help find out who really was responsible for the bombing threat.

"But Mr. Zeering didn't believe them and took them as prisoners. I thought he was right until I saw you coming across that meadow with those sticks of dynamite.

"What were you going to do — plant them at the hermit's before going on to really blow up the dam and get him blamed?"

Rulon spoke scornfully. "You're the smart one, ain't you?"

Alfred protested, "Don't mind him! He's probably a little bit out of his head from almost drowning—"

D.J. interrupted. "Of course!" He turned to face the Krockners. "You didn't have the bail money! So you got it from someone — the Thorkells!"

Alfred groaned. "Aw, D.J."

D.J. plunged on, seeing things more clearly. "All four of you were in it together, weren't you? It was the Thorkells' idea, but they needed you to help out! And probably they'd later have left you two holding the bag while they skipped out, free and clear!"

Beau Krockner sighed slowly. "You're right every way. And me'n Rulon already figgered out that them radical environmental people was a'goin' to frame us, same's they framed the hermit."

"But why?"

Beau shrugged. "Money — what else? We met the Thorkells in the woods once. They said they wanted to play a little joke on a friend."

"The hermit," D.J. guessed.

"Yep! We was just supposed to put a half box of

dynamite in the old man's shack. Wasn't supposed
to be dangerous without blasting caps to set it off."

"So we done it," Rulon added. "Later, them
Thorkells gave us money to bail the hermit out of
jail, plus some extra money for our trouble.
Thorkells also hired the lawyer."

Beau said, "Now you figured it out. But what're
you a'goin' to do—seeing as how we saved your
life?"

D.J. was silent for a long time. He glanced at Alfred, whose wide eyes behind his thick glasses
showed he was totally surprised by the unexpected
turn of events.

"I don't know," he said softly. "I'll think about it
while we're climbing out of here to a phone."

The senior Krockner pursed his lips thoughtfully.
"You do that. That's all I ask. You boys go on up the
hill. Me'n my boy will go off by ourselves."

D.J. protested weakly, "I can't let you do that!"

"How you a'goin' to stop us?" Rulon demanded.

Alfred reached out and touched D.J.'s bare, muddy arm. "You promised your folks you'd let the
sheriff handle things. Remember? Let them go!"

D.J. told the Krockners, "I can't stop you. But the
deputies will catch up with you, sooner or later."

"Maybe," Beau said through his muddy beard.
"Maybe not. We'll take our chances. What d'ya say?"

D.J. shrugged. "What can I say—except thanks
again for pulling me out of that mud."

Chapter Thirteen

EASTER SUNDAY

Before sunup Easter morning, the parking lot was full at Lookout Peak. Under a cold, crisp, clear sky, D.J. and his family made their way along the folded chairs set up near the foot of the cross.

D.J. was very stiff and sore under the heavy coat, so it was hard to move. He wished he'd brought a blanket to wrap himself in, as his father, stepmother, stepsister, and grandfather had. They sat on D.J.'s right in the second row from the front.

He could hardly wait until after this service so he could phone the vet to find out how Hero was doing. Last night, when D.J. had checked, there was no change. Infection from his terrible wounds still threatened the little dog's life.

D.J. shook off the thought and smiled when Kathy and her mother walked in, wearing heavy coats and each carrying a blanket. They took seats in the front row while Brother Paul in his topcoat moved forward to check the microphone.

D.J. had forgotten to go back to the dime store and get the Easter cards he'd left when he'd heard Hero being attacked. The boy had bought one card each for Two Mom and Mrs. Stagg. *Oh well,* D.J. thought. *I'll give them the cards later—they'll understand.*

Alfred slid in beside D.J. on the left. He was followed by his parents and little brother. D.J. nodded to the Milfords as Alfred leaned close.

"You hear the news?"

"What news?" D.J. asked from where he'd drawn his chin inside his upturned coat collar.

"The Thorkells confessed to the deputies."

"They did?"

"Sure did! It was on the car radio as we drove up. The announcer said the authorities expect that radical environmentalist, Thorkell, to be in jail for a long time. His son Thad is being held in juvenile hall. Something about federal laws being broken in making bomb threats."

"What about the Krockners?"

Alfred shrugged. "After we reported the accident to the sheriff's office, the deputies followed the Krockners' trail along the canyon wall and into the mud that poured over the top there. They apparently tried to cut across it, but their trail disappeared as completely as their dogs did."

For a second, D.J. glanced at Two Mom, remembering what she had quoted from the Bible: " 'Vengeance is Mine; I will repay,' saith the Lord" (Romans 12:19).

His thoughts were interrupted as someone

touched his shoulder from behind. He turned around. For a second, he didn't recognize Dr. Barner. She was warmly clad in a zippered gray jacket and leather gloves.

She said, "I brought my mother to the services, D.J., and I just happened to see you. Your dog—"

D.J. nearly died as the lady vet hesitated, then added, "I stopped at the hospital on the way up here. Hero's out of danger!"

D.J. jumped up. "He is?"

Tears sprang to the boy's eyes as the lady vet nodded. Alfred jumped up and happily thumped D.J.'s left shoulder. Two Mom, Dad, and the rest of his family leaned over and grinned at him.

Brother Paul's deep voice boomed from the two black portable loudspeakers. "Please find your seats, folks!"

Dr. Barner excused herself and hurried away to find a seat just as the first rays of the sun sent long, warm fingers across the sky. D.J. wanted to shout, "Hero's OK! He's going to live!" Instead, he automatically obeyed the lay preacher and sat down. D.J. saw Mrs. Stagg and Kathy smiling at him from the front row.

Kathy leaned over and whispered, "We're happy for you, D.J. But it's too bad about those radical environmentalists! Such people hurt all of us who are genuinely concerned about our environment!"

D.J. nodded just as the lay pastor's powerful voice rumbled up from his deep chest and echoed off into the distance.

"This is Resurrection morning! The day we observe because the Lord was dead and buried

—and rose again. Let's celebrate the risen Saviour by opening our hymnbooks to number 128."

D.J. stood with the others, but he didn't sing. The meaning of Easter overwhelmed him in a way he had never known before. He thought of the report he'd stayed up late last night to write for Mrs. Stagg's Sunday School class. He was sure she'd like it.

His thoughts evaporated as he saw the hermit of Mad River entering the parking lot. D.J. realized the old man had climbed the deer trail up the mountain, past the mud slide area.

He had shaved and dressed in a very old blue suit with an out-of-style yellow polka-dot tie. The hermit's uncut hair was neatly combed.

D.J. squeezed past the Milfords and hurried toward the old man. " 'Morning, Mr. Zeering," D.J. said with a smile. "Come sit with me."

The old man's eyes misted. He grabbed the boy's hands in both of his. "I'd be right proud to do that, D.J."

They walked side by side toward the singing congregation. The people smiled greetings and Mr. Zeering bobbed his head in solemn reply. The people in D.J.'s row made room for them. D.J. seated the hermit between Alfred and himself.

Two Mom handed her hymnal to the old man, but he shook his head and began singing heartily from memory. D.J. was startled. He hadn't dreamed that Mr. Zeering might remember a song from so long ago.

From now on, Easter is going to be special to me! D.J. told himself happily. *Very special!*

* * * * *

More exciting adventures are waiting for D.J. and Alfred. Read about them in the next D.J. Dillon adventure, **Escape Down the Raging Rapids.**

LIFE IN STONEY RIDGE

ADOBE: Sun-dried bricks made of moist clay (as from a river). The dried bricks kept houses and stores warm in the winter and cool in the summer.

ANTIBIOTICS: Any of a group of chemical substances, including penicillin, used to treat infectious diseases.

ASPIRATED: To remove fluid from a part of the body by suction.

BLASTING CAPS: Small explosive devices used to set off dynamite.

BRINDLED: Boog was tawny, or a dull yellowish-brown color with prominent darker streaks. Brindles may also be gray and have spots.

CALICO CAT: A domestic cat, usually female, of variegated yellow, black, and white coloring.

CATALPA: A shade tree found in California's foothills. The catalpa has very large leaves and bell-shaped white flowers.

CONIFERS: Another name for the many cone-bearing trees or shrubs. Spruce, fir, and pine trees are all conifers.

COON'S AGE: Slang expression meaning a very long time, since raccoons were once believed to have long lives.

CORRUGATED: A type of metal with alternating ridges and grooves that make it sturdy.

DOUBLE-BITTED AX HEAD: An ax that has two cutting edges instead of one.

DOUBLE-OUGHT BUCKSHOT: Large pellets from a shotgun.

DOUGLAS FIR: A large forest tree growing up to 300 feet tall, erroneously called Oregon pine. Douglas fir is considered the most important lumber tree. It has cones 2 to 4 inches long. Young trees are typically pyramidal at the crown with horizontal and sometimes drooping, lacy branches. A pretty tree, the mature branches tend to become rounded or somewhat flattened. Small Douglas firs are commonly used as Christmas trees.

DURESS: The force or threat used to make a person do something he doesn't want to do.

FEDORA: A soft felt hat with crown creased lengthwise and a curled brim.

HACKLES: The hair on a dog's neck and back that stands up when the dog is angry or afraid.

HAIR-PULLING BEAR DOG: A small, quick dog of mixed breed. A hair-puller's natural tendency is to go for the heels or backside of any animal, including sheep, cows, or bears.

IMPOUNDED: To confine or hold within limits.

INCENSE CEDAR: A type of fragrant coniferous tree.

IRISH SHILLELAGH (pronounced "Shuh-LAY-Lee"): A cudgel or short, thick stick often used for a walking cane. A shillelagh is usually made of blackthorn saplings or oak and is named after the Irish village of Shillelagh.

MAGAZINE CONTEST: The story of how D.J. won the typewriter is told in Book 2, **The Bear Cub Disaster.**

MANZANITA: A thickly branched bush. Its small leaves have smooth edges with white fuzz on their undersurface. The manzanita bush has twisted and gnarled maroon-colored limbs that burn very hot in a fire. Manzanita may grow as tall as 20 feet and can provide thick cover for bears and other animals.

MASTIFF CROSS: A mastiff is a breed of big, strong, short-haired dogs. This particular dog was mixed or crossed with another unknown breed.

MOTHER LODE: A term applied to the gold-bearing area in the foothill section of California's Sierra Nevada Mountains running from about Mariposa on the south (near Yosemite) to Downieville in the north. The famous Gold Rush of 1849 covered this area. Many people still find gold today in the Mother Lode.

MOUNTAIN MISERY: A low-growing, fernlike mountain plant that gives off a bad smell when it is touched or walked on. The plant is full of resin which explodes in a fire. Because of this, forestry personnel usually burn it to keep it under control. Mountain misery, also called "bear clover," has a pretty white flower which looks like snow. *Kitkit dizze* is the Indian name for mountain misery.

'NAM: A short form of the name of Vietnam, a country in southeastern Asia. Vietnam was the site of American military action in the late 1960s and early 1970s.

OL' SATCHELFOOT: An outlaw bear that was told about in the first D.J. Dillon adventure, **The Hair-Pulling Bear Dog.**

PALM SUNDAY: The Sunday before Easter. It celebrates Jesus' entry into Jerusalem where the people waved palm branches.

PONDEROSA PINES: Large North American trees used for lumber. Ponderosa pines usually grow in the mountain regions of the West and can reach heights of 200 feet. The ponderosa pine is the state tree of Montana.

POWDER MONKEY: A person in charge of explosives.

QUARTERING TROT: The term given to the way a dog's legs move when he trots—seemingly not straight ahead, but slightly to one side, about a quarter of the way off-center.

RECOGNIZANCE: In law, a binding obligation before a court to do a certain act—as in Own Recognizance (O.R.), when a person released is responsible on his own.

SAWDUST TRAIL: A slang expression meaning a person has taken steps toward getting right with God. The term apparently developed from the days when sawdust was used to keep down the dust on the ground where outdoor religious meetings were held. Someone responding to an altar call at such a meeting was said to be "hitting the sawdust trail."

SHANTY: A crudely-built small structure, such as a cabin.

SHRAPNEL: A military term for fragments from an exploding shell.

SNAG: A short stump of a tree that had been broken off.

STETSON: A broad-brimmed, high-crowned felt hat like a cowboy's. The Stetson is named for John B. Stetson, an American hatmaker who lived during the time of the Old West.

STRINGER: A journalism term for a part-time newspaper correspondent who covers his own local area for a paper published somewhere else.

SUGAR PINES: Largest of the pine trees. Sugar pines can grow as tall as 240 feet. They have cones that range from 10 to 26 inches long which are often used for decoration.

TAMP: To pack in tightly by lightly tapping with repeated strokes.

TETCHED IN THE HEAD: A slang expression for "touched," or not mentally quite right.

TISSUE TRAUMA: A veterinarian's term for a severe injury to the fleshy part of an animal. *Trauma* is from the Greek word for wound.

D.J. DILLON
· ADVENTURE SERIES ·

The Hair-Pulling Bear Dog
D.J.'s ugly mutt gets a chance to prove his courage.

The Bear Cub Disaster
When his pet bear causes trouble in Stoney Ridge, D.J. realizes he can't keep the cub forever.

Dooger, The Grasshopper Hound
D.J. and his buddy Alfred rely on an untrained hound to save Alfred's little brother from a forest fire.

The Ghost Dog of Stoney Ridge
D.J. and Alfred find out what's polluting the mountain lakes — and end up solving the ghost dog mystery.

Mad Dog of Lobo Mountain
D.J. struggles to save his dog's life and learns a hard lesson about responsibility.

The Legend of the White Raccoon
Is the white raccoon real or only a phantom? As D.J. tries to find out, he stumbles upon a dangerous secret.

The Mystery of the Black Hole Mine
D.J. battles "gold" fever, and learns an eye-opening lesson about his own selfishness and greed.

Ghost of the Moaning Mansion

Will D.J. and Alfred get scared away from the moaning mansion before they find the "real" ghost?

The Secret of Mad River

D.J.'s dog is an innocent victim — and so is the hermit of Mad River. Can D.J. prove the hermit's innocence before it's too late?

Escape Down the Raging Rapids

D.J.'s life depends on reaching a doctor soon, but forest fires and the dangerous raging rapids of Mad River stand in his way.

*Look for these exciting stories
at your local Christian bookstore.*